MOONSHINE & MASQUERADES

MOONSHINE HOLLOW #6

KATHLEEN BROOKS

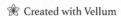 Created with Vellum

Forever Concealed

Forever Devoted

Forever Hunted

Forever Guarded

Forever Notorious

Forever Ventured

Forever Freed

Forever Saved

Forever Bold

Forever Thrown

Forever Lies (coming Jan/Feb 2022)

Shadows Landing Series

Saving Shadows

Sunken Shadows

Lasting Shadows

Fierce Shadows

Broken Shadows

Framed Shadows

Endless Shadows

Fading Shadows (coming April/May 2022)

Women of Power Series

Chosen for Power

Built for Power

Fashioned for Power

Destined for Power

1

Zoey stared at the mixing bowl in the early morning darkness. The town had gone home after a mountainous wave of blood tried to take out all the citizens in the park the night before. The people of Moonshine Hollow had almost been killed, they'd learned about witches, and now the Claritase, the female witches, and the Tenebris, the male witches, waited to hear the results from a town meeting being held that afternoon—a meeting that Zoey nor any other witch was invited to. Today the town decided not only their own fate, but also the fate of all the witches in the small town of Moonshine Hollow.

Grand Mistress Lauren, the leader of the Claritase, had given the town three options. One, the witches would erase their memories. Life would go on as if they hadn't been tormented by an evil witch practicing dark magic and they wouldn't know the influx of new residents in the small town of Moonshine Hollow were all witches. Two, they'd vote for all the witches to leave and never come back. Or three, they'd vote to live among the witches, knowing they were in the middle of a magical battle between good and evil that humans could never win on their own.

Every witch was blessed with a power rooted in the elements: earth, air, water, or fire. However, Zoey had somehow inherited the fifth element. The Greeks believed it was the pure essence that the gods lived on. Aristotle called it *æther* and he believed it was the first element, the element that created all other elements. Zoey's element was neither wet nor dry, nor was it hot or cold. It was neither light nor dark. It simply absorbed all Zoey told it to. Modern scientists call it dark energy as it is both nothingness and all.

Zoey hadn't been able to sleep after she left the park last night. Her father, Magnus Rode, was missing and presumed to have had given his life for them. He'd held off the tsunami of blood that was barreling down on the town to give Zoey and the other witch leaders time to join with the other witches and protect the town.

Zoey hadn't been able to sleep so she'd come to her bakery, Zoey's Sweet Treats. Her black Labrador, Chance, accompanied her. In these early morning hours, she mixed the batter for the muffins that used to feed the town each day. Now she didn't know if anyone would even show up when she opened.

Normally, early mornings at the bakery gave her time to mediate. She felt close to the Goddess as she reached out with her powers to ensure the safety of all the residents, human and witch alike. Zoey tried to focus this morning and reach out with her powers.

Instead of feeling the goodness in people, she felt the anger, the distrust, and the desire for revenge. Zoey dropped her hands and opened her eyes. What was happening to her?

"You've been tainted by the black magic."

"Oh my Goddess!" Zoey jumped and spun around to face the intruder. "You have got to stop doing that."

Grand Mistress Lauren just shrugged one shoulder. She wasn't going to stop just popping into the bakery's kitchen. It was kind of her thing now.

"What do you mean I'm tainted by black magic?" Zoey asked, now worried after her initial scare of Lauren popping in on her.

"Jane is too. I'm willing to bet you all are. You six were the ones holding it off the longest. Did you feel it reaching for you?" Lauren asked as she took a seat on the stool by the mixer and grabbed a muffin fresh from the oven. Lauren may be the grand mistress, but when you looked at her you just saw a put together forty year old. She was confident, rocked her casual, yet professional clothes, and her black hair was always perfect.

"I did. I felt it sliding over my powers."

"We need to go to the stones. Galen should be feeling better by this afternoon and can help heal you. It's his thing after all," Lauren said with a sad smile. Galen was the Keeper of the Stones of Stenness, basically the doctor to the magical powers of witches.

"What is it? Did something more happen?" Zoey asked. She crossed her arms over her chest and tried not to pace nervously around the kitchen.

"I failed," Lauren said. She turned her head away from Zoey so Zoey wouldn't see the tears. "Your father is missing, we've been exposed to the town, the evil is growing stronger, and we can't figure out the connections between The Six that the prophecy tells us will help us defeat the evil."

Zoey placed her hand on Lauren's arm. Their grand mistress had kept the Claritase protected the best she could for four hundred years while the evil Hunters tried to steal their powers. She'd helped train Zoey and she was going to lead them into their future. "Maybe you need to go to the stones with us. There's no one else I rather have as our leader."

"I'll do that. Thank you for inviting me."

"In fact, I think the whole council should go," Zoey told her.

"A retreat. That would be nice. First we'll see what the town votes. We'll deal with that and then head to the stones. We can work on the connection between The Six together. *A traitor, a love taken, families destroyed all for power. A masquerade hiding evil has been in place too long. It's time to reveal who is under the mask. Only a power stronger than True Love can defeat the dark magic as evil as this.*" Lauren recited the prophecy from Slade's mother, the past grand mistress.

"*Only together can you stop it. Fate has played her last hand,*" Zoey said, finishing the prophecy. She remembered the image of The Six—Zoey, Slade, Polly, Samuel, Jane, and Galen—standing trapped in the middle of the bridge in the park. She remembered the way the blood rain fell and the shadows converging on them from both sides as the town of Moonshine Hollow burned to the ground. That was the prophecy they'd been given. That was the responsibility Zoey had weighing on her shoulders.

"Does it really matter why we're connected? It could just be because we're friends," Zoey said as she went back to baking. She'd do anything to get the screams of pain she'd heard when the prophecy was revealed to them out of her head.

"I'm best friends with Neferu, yet we're not in the vision. I think it has to do with the future. Either I'm dead when this battle happens or it's a sign that you six are to lead us into the future."

Zoey shook her head. "I don't think so. I think it's personal, very personal. It's just a feeling I have since the prophecy talked about very personal things like being a traitor, a love dying, and families destroyed. If it is personal, then it's very important for us to figure out the connection the six of us have in order to solve who is using black magic."

"Masquerade hiding evil . . ." Lauren said slowly. "Could that mean someone is pretending to be good, but is really bad?"

"A traitor," Zoey said as her mind rolled it over.

"Exactly, a traitor. We need to get to the stones as fast as possible."

"Then let's handle the breakfast rush so these humans can get their vote over with," Agnes said from behind Zoey.

Zoey jumped in surprise and placed her hand over her heart. "Would you stop that!"

"Stop what?"

Zoey jumped again as Vilma *poofed* in behind her again. Zoey spun around and saw the two old witches smiling with amusement. Zoey wanted to be mad, but they were smiling and having such fun at scaring her she could only laugh. "It's a good thing I love you both so much or I'd zap you."

"Could be fun," Agnes said to Vilma.

"I wonder if it still tingles," Vilma responded and even Grand Mistress Lauren began to laugh. "Seriously though, we're here to help get you ready to open and then I agree, the councils need to go to the stones. We need to meditate, talk it all out, and get to the bottom of this now."

Zoey nodded as Vilma flicked her wrist and fresh flowers appeared on all the tables. Agnes wiggled her fingers and a mop went to work on the floors. It was almost like they'd talked about it and planned it, but they didn't say one word about the town meeting that was being held in two hours. They didn't talk about the prophecy or evil witches. They just got ready for the day like they did every other day.

"So," Grand Mistress Lauren said mischievously, "anything you want to tell us, Zoey?"

Zoey groaned and then threw a muffin at the leader of all the Claritase. "I am not pregnant! But . . ." Zoey waited until Lauren looked as if she couldn't stand the suspense anymore. "I think it's time . . ." Lauren gasped and clapped her hands together in celebration of future witchlings, "for you to get married. You've been single for way too many centuries, Grand Mistress."

Zoey struggled not to laugh as Lauren's excited expression fell into shock and confusion. "What?"

"You should get married," Zoey said with a smile. "And have witchlings. Lots and lots of witchlings."

The shocked look on Lauren's face made all the darkness fall away. Zoey was laughing so hard her whole spirit was lifted.

"That's not funny," Lauren said, crossing her arms.

"Hey, if you dish it out, be prepared to have it shoveled back at you," Agnes said from where she was wiping tears of laughter from her eyes.

"It's not that I wouldn't like all of that. I just don't know if I'll have a second chance at True Love. And, as grand mistress, I think I intimidate a lot of the Tenebris."

"Now we have a mission. Well, after we save the fate of our kind and the citizens of Moonshine Hollow. Then we have another mission—finding your True Love." Zoey looked to Agnes and Vilma who were already looking at Agnes's cell phone.

"We can make you a profile on WitchMatch.com in the

meantime. Smile." Agnes snapped a horrible photo of Lauren in a mid-*You did what?* Look. Lauren was horrified, Zoey couldn't stop giggling, and Agnes and Vilma were so focused on the dating app for witches that had popped up after Alexander was killed they didn't notice Lauren moving to see what they were writing.

"Age: One thousand is the new one hundred," Lauren read off the phone. "Sex: It's been so long I've forgotten how."

Zoey snorted. She covered her nose, but somehow ended up snorting again anyway. She was laughing so hard she distracted Agnes and Vilma long enough for Lauren to grab the phone and frantically start deleting the profile.

"Wow."

"Wow, what?" Agnes said, trying to use magic to get her phone back.

"Look at this guy," Lauren turned the phone around and everyone went silent.

He looked around Lauren's age, well, the human age she appeared to be, and he was shirtless. For that matter, he was bottomless, too.

The women looked from the picture to each other and burst out laughing again. "I don't think they should be shaped like that," Vilma said, snatching the phone and turning it sideways. "Maybe I should tell him to see a doctor."

They were laughing so hard that Zoey almost missed the knock on the front door. She peered out from the kitchen and was surprised to find a line down the sidewalk. "Well, here we go."

2

Zoey opened the door to the bakery. She gave an uncertain smile to her best friend, Maribelle, who was first in line. Maribelle looked into the bakery and waved. "Zoey, Agnes, Vilma, and Lauren are here," Maribelle called out to the long line. "You might want to use some of that magic of yours to feed us all so you have time to answer all our questions before the meeting starts."

With that, Maribelle walked into the bakery followed by most of the town. Miss Moonshine wore her crown and sash, the Irises brought baked goods, their husbands in the Opossums brought mason jars of moonshine, and the Mountaineers, the club for the younger set, brought nothing but their curiosity and tentative smiles.

"We only have an hour until the meeting. Everyone take whatever it is Zoey gives you and give her five bucks. No change today. We've got to move it along here, people," Maribelle called out with more confidence and leadership than Zoey had ever seen from her friend before.

People went through the line taking all the muffins she had and tossing their money on the counter in a flurry of motion. In less than ten minutes, Zoey sold out of everything she had.

"Aw, I really wanted a muffin," Nancy sighed.

"I don't have time to make regular muffins, but I can *make* one now if you don't mind," Zoey said to her.

"You mean a magical muffin? Will I get high?" Nancy asked as everyone in line behind her leaned forward.

"No," Zoey laughed. "It'll taste just like a regular muffin because it will be a regular muffin. Just made a lot quicker."

"And I won't get high?" Nancy asked again.

"I don't mind if I get high," her husband told Zoey.

"No one will get high," Zoey said loud enough for the rest of the people to hear.

"I'll try one," Nancy finally said.

Zoey wiggled her fingers and a muffin appeared in Nancy's hand. The bakery was quiet as they all watched Nancy raise the muffin to her mouth. She paused with the muffin near her mouth and stared at it for a moment. Then, as if mentally hyping herself up, she finally took a bite. "Hmmm. It tastes just the same. Are you sure I can't fly or something? That would be really cool."

"I'm sure you can't fly. Does anyone else want one?" Zoey asked. Most of the people in line nodded and Zoey wiggled her fingers and muffins appeared in their hands. "So, what can we do for you all?"

"We have questions and we need answers so we can make an informed decision for the town vote," Maribelle said, clearly the leader of this large group. "Mr. Earnest wants us to all discuss the situation and then we'll vote. However, I didn't see how we could properly discuss it without knowing all the facts. As you can see, most of us are reasonable like that. Others, not so much."

"I think it's a very wise course of action," Agnes said,

coming to stand next to Zoey. Vilma and Lauren stepped up as well. They were a panel of Claritase ready to face this onslaught of questions together.

"I collected a list of questions," Maribelle said, holding up a list. "The first one, can you use mind control on us?"

Lauren raised her hand as if in class. "I'll take this. We will answer everything honestly, even if it's the answer you don't want to hear. Yes, we can use mind control or alter your thoughts. But not every Circe, Morgana, and Merlin can do it. It takes a powerful witch. It's also completely against everything we believe. When it's been done to the residents of Moonshine Hollow, it was to protect our existence and our people—the women who were captured by the Hunters for example. You have to understand that for centuries we have been killed on the spot for being real witches. You are the first group of humans we've ever shared our secrets with. So, to really answer your question. Yes, we can make bad things seem like a dream. Powerful witches can use mind control. That means us, who won't do it without your permission, and also bad witches who would never ask permission."

Nancy raised her hand. "So, there's like different levels of witches?"

"Yes. Family lines have a large role in how strong your powers are. Zoey's father for example," Lauren stopped as she caught herself.

"Has he been found?" Nancy asked quietly.

"Not yet." Zoey felt the tears threatening, but tried to push them back. "What Lauren was saying is that my father's line is very strong. My mother is a human, yet the line is so powerful that it has made me one of the most powerful witches in history."

"Slade's mother was a former grand mistress, so he's

very powerful. The Farrington line, the Kendrick line—those are Jane's parents'—are very strong. They're all originals. There are several others too. Then there are some that are very strong in certain areas," Lauren explained. "Like very strong in healing or foresight for example."

"Are there still Hunters?" Maribelle asked from the list.

"We're sure there are, but we don't know who they are. Whoever is behind what happened here this week could be a Hunter. We just don't know yet," Vilma answered.

"Do you fly on broomsticks?" Maribelle asked.

Zoey snickered and the rest rolled their eyes. "No!" they all said together.

"We can transport, though," Agnes said and then *poofed* away and reappeared a minute later with a bottle of Italian wine. "I just grabbed this from a winery in Tuscany."

Agnes set the bottle of wine on the table and everyone stared at it in wonder. The next hour was spent in rapid-fire questioning. Their powers were explained, their philosophy and moral code were explained, their history was told, they swore they didn't wear pointy hats, and finally they landed on the main points.

"What will happen to the town if this dark magic comes back?" Maribelle asked. The laughter died down as things grew serious again.

"Well, if we're here, we will do everything we can to protect you and the town just like we did last night. If you give us permission to be here and promise to never share this information with anyone, we can be out in the open to fight this evil. The fact is, if we stay, the war will come to us," Zoey answered honestly. "I can't say whether or not whoever they are will still attack the town if we're not here. But if they do, you won't have a chance."

"The person could mind control us to do bad things, right?" Nancy asked.

"Yes. It's been done before," Zoey said as she recounted the men who had come to kidnap Jane for Ian. "But if we're here, we can counteract the mind control."

Lauren sighed and gave an exhausted smile. "This is a lot to process in such a short time. We will always try to look out for you, even if we're not here. We want you to be comfortable with whatever you decide."

Doris, the tough as nails secretary for the health clinic, didn't bother raising her hand. She just glared at her watch and then at the witches. "What's to stop you from using mind control to make us forget all of this and just go back to the way it was?"

"Nothing," Lauren said honestly, "Nothing but the fact that I gave you my word that I'd let you decide your fate. I'm going to live up to it. We are going to live up to it."

"What can you give us if we let you stay?" Doris asked bluntly.

"Well, we're not going to bribe you, Doris," Vilma said just as bluntly. "It'll be just how it has been for all the years Agnes and I have lived here. We'll help where and when we can. More so now that you know we have powers and we won't have to come up with a lie. However, we're not going to steal money and we're not going to give you unfair advantages. We might help with your garden though. It's truly a crime what you do to those poor flowers."

Zoey couldn't believe it. Doris's flat, thin, and hard-pressed lips quirked up into a small smile. Then it was gone just as fast as it appeared.

"So, we have to trust you to not harm us," Billy Ray said. Zoey could see his mind working through all of this.

"And we have to trust you not to harm us," Lauren answered just as quickly.

"It's time to go," Doris said into the silence.

Maribelle smiled nervously at them. "Thank you for being so honest with us and answering our questions." People started to leave and Maribelle wrapped Zoey in a hug. "I'll text you to let you know what's going on."

"Thank you. You're a good friend, Maribelle," Zoey whispered back.

The bakery and the sidewalk, where the open door had allowed people on the sidewalk to hear the conversations, started to clear. The last person to leave was Doris. The formidable woman walked over to Zoey and looked her straight in the eye. "I'd love the name of the shop Slade gets his leather pants from. When you have time." Then Doris turned around and strode from the room.

"That was the most disturbing part of this day so far," Zoey muttered as Agnes, Vilma, and Lauren broke out into peals of laughter.

"Well, the town is meeting. I think we should too. Your backyard in five." With that Lauren disappeared and Zoey knew the witch text chain would be blowing up any second.

"You better whip up some more muffins. You know we can be real witches when we don't get breakfast." Agnes winked at her and then *poofed* away.

"You did good, kid. We'll see what hand fate deals us and we'll tackle it head on. Oh," Vilma added, a second before she *poofed* away, "the double chocolate chip muffins would be perfect."

3

Slade and Samuel got the message about gathering as they held their morning meeting at the sheriff's department. Their human staff had not shown up for work, which wasn't surprising.

"I wonder if the grand mistress will understand this feeling of being off we have," Samuel said to Slade as they stood up. Instead of transporting, they decided to walk the short distance to Slade and Zoey's home.

"I hope so. She's a strong healer after all. My stomach is a mess and I feel as if my True Love bond is off. Well"— Slade fought to think of the right way to describe it as he locked the door— "it feels different, that's all."

"I have the same feeling. I also feel sluggish. And look at my powers." Samuel called his powers forward and formed a ball of air energy in his hands. "It's gray, not light blue."

Slade called up his powers and frowned. "Mine's a deep purple, almost black, when it should be a royal purple."

Samuel sighed. "Something has changed with Polly too. She didn't want to get out of bed this morning and that is not like her."

"Zoey had insomnia. She didn't sleep at all. I heard her sneak out of the house to go to the bakery early this morning. As if anyone would show up this morning," Slade said with a scoff.

Slade and Samuel talked until they reached the house. Witches looked morose as they walked around to the back of the house. For four hundred years, they'd been in hiding from humans and other witches. They finally found a place to call home and be with friends and family again and then this happens. The war they thought was over was, in fact, far from over. It had taken their second grand master in less than a year from them. Slade could tell by the downcast eyes and shuffling feet that everyone expected to be on the run once again.

The only reason he didn't think they would leave was because of the vision shown to them by his mother and Linus. It was clear they would make their last stand in Moonshine Hollow. What was less clear was whether or not they would live through it.

Slade immediately found Zoey in the crowd. The shimmer she'd had seemed dulled today. Another sign something wasn't right.

"How are you feeling?" Slade asked as he pulled his True Love to him and placed a kiss on the top of her head.

"Confused. Lauren said I have been tainted by black magic. She wants us all to go to the stones to be cleansed."

"My powers feel darker, so that makes sense."

"The humans came to see us this morning."

Slade looked down in surprise at Zoey. "They did?"

"I'd say about two-thirds of them did. They packed into the bakery and onto the street. Maribelle organized it. They'd submitted questions and we answered them all for over an hour. Maribelle is going to text us during the meeting too."

"She's a good friend," Slade said, sliding his hand down Zoey's back and absently rubbing his thumb up and down her spine.

Lauren stepped to the front of the crowd. Witches filled every corner of Zoey's large backyard. No one was smiling.

"Maribelle is going to keep us updated as the humans' meeting progresses. A large number of Moonshiners came to talk to us this morning, so I can only hope that's good news. However, I have also noticed in our effort to fend off the black magic we've all been tainted by it." Lauren waited as witches talked to each other and a number of them called their powers forward and then exclaimed at seeing them muted in color. "We will wait for the town's decision. Then we will go to the stones in shifts. Galen and Jane have just left to get everything ready for a cleansing ritual. We'll have to go in shifts, so expect it to be a long day. We will leave the majority of witches here in case there are any issues. That way the town will have a defense until the others can get back."

Everyone nodded and Slade heard Zoey's phone buzz with an incoming message. She looked down at it and when she looked up, Slade saw the entire Claritase and Tenebris watching her with worried eyes.

"The meeting has started. Mr. Earnest is talking now. Then they'll open it up for people to go up and speak. So far thirteen people have signed up to speak. Maribelle said she'll take the last spot," Zoey told the group.

And so they waited. Zoey and Slade moved to join Lauren so they could give updates. Well, so Zoey could. Slade moved to stand next to Lauren since he was technically grand master. He didn't feel like he was though. It couldn't end like this for Magnus.

Zoey's phone buzzed and everyone instantly went quiet. "Maribelle is about to speak. So far she says the worst damage was done by Clara."

Zoey's phone rang and she put it on speaker. "Maribelle?"

No one replied though. Every witch leaned forward to hear, but things were muffled until Maribelle's voice came across strong and clear.

"Excuse me for using my phone, but my notes are on it. First, I was elected by a group of over five hundred citizens to speak on their behalf," Maribelle's clear voice came through.

"What's going on?" Slade whispered as Zoey moved to quickly mute her phone.

Zoey's heart filled with love for her friend. "She's letting us hear her speech. Everyone, quiet!"

Zoey held her breath as Maribelle's voice came over the phone. She could only shake her head at Slade as she waited for Maribelle's next words. She didn't dare answer Slade as she didn't want to miss a word Maribelle said.

"Zoey is my best friend. But I am not the only one lucky enough to call her my friend. Every morning we go to her bakery, we eat her food, and we share our mornings together. In the past year, Zoey has saved me from jail, been by my side through thick and thin, and has shown not only me, but also all of you, how much Moonshine Hollow means to her.

"Then there's Agnes and Vilma, two women who have helped this town in more ways than we can ever count or thank them for. I have spent every hour since we left the park yesterday talking to as many people as I could. One thing they all had in common was that Agnes and Velma had helped them at some point in their lives when they thought it was hopeless.

"When evil was upon us last night, it was the witches who protected us, just like Agnes, Velma, and Zoey have protected us in the past. I'm aware that evil would not have come to Moonshine Hollow if not for the witches. However, every single person here has been touched for the better because of them. Now it's our turn to help them.

"This morning hundreds of us went to Zoey's bakery to speak to her. Instead of secrecy, Zoey, Lauren, Agnes, and Vilma answered all of our questions and faced all of our concerns head-on. They did not lie to us, they did not downplay the seriousness of the situation, but they did share their love for not only us but for the entire town as well. They promise to protect us and I believe that they will. You have heard Nancy speak in support of them, and you have heard Doris speak passionately about how Lauren and the other witches have helped the patients of Moonshine Hollow, and now you'll hear the truth, straight from the witches' mouths. Here are the questions we had and here are their answers."

Zoey finally breathed again as Maribelle read a summary from their morning meeting. Her speech went on for another thirty minutes until she concluded with the history of Moonshine Hollow.

"We started as a tight knit community in the wilderness. We all learned the lessons of our ancestors: to be neighborly, to stand for what is right, and to never back down when someone tries to take what's yours. Well, Moonshine Hollow is ours and it's under attack. Our friends and neighbors are under attack. There's nothing more to say except it's the right thing to do. We should stand up to evil, stare it in the eyes, and shoot the miserable bastard in the heart for messing with the town and people we love."

Zoey heard cheers and clapping as Maribelle grabbed the phone and walked off stage. The phone was turned off then and Zoey almost cried with grief.

"Maribelle is right. We don't run from evil. We fight it," Zoey said into the silent crowd, her voice rising along with her passion to defeat the being trying to take everything from them. "I for one vow to fight this evil until one of us dies and it won't be me. Who's with me?"

"I'm with you," Slade said, reaching out and grabbing her hand.

"I'm with you," Polly said, reaching out and taking Zoey's other hand.

"I'm with you," Samuel said, taking his wife's hand in his.

One by one, each witch stepped forward and agreed to make a stand against evil. They linked hands with the person at the end of the line and soon the winding circle of witches stood hand in hand together and made a vow to the Goddess, to their friends, to the town, and to themselves that no matter what they'd protect the innocent and never back down from evil.

Zoey felt her phone vibrate and looked down at the text message. "The town has asked that we join them in the park."

"Do we walk or . . ." Samuel asked.

"Well, they know we're witches and I'm quite eager to hear the news," Lauren said a second before *poofing* away.

Zoey shrugged and in seconds all the witches of Moonshine Hollow were in the park. They were behind the humans who were facing the stage. "You asked to see us?" Lauren called out. Several humans jumped in surprise. Maybe it wasn't the best way to endear them to witches, but Lauren was right. If they allowed them to stay, the town might need to get used to seeing the odd power here or there.

"Um, yes," Mr. Earnest said into the microphone on the stage. "I'm glad you were able to join us so quickly. We thought you'd want to know the results of the vote. But first, we have one final question."

Lauren nodded her head as if to tell him to go ahead and ask.

"Why would you stay? Why wouldn't you run to hide from whatever was so powerful they could do what they did last night?"

Lauren stood up straight and looked every inch the powerful leader she was. "Because it's the right thing to do. Just before you contacted us, every witch here vowed to give their life to protect the innocent from this evil, and we intend to fulfill that vow."

Mr. Earnest nodded and Maribelle blew Zoey a kiss from where she stood near the stage. "The results are in and there was a clear mandate. Ninety-two percent of the town agrees." Mr. Earnest paused and Zoey could zap him for doing so. Her heart was pounding and her stomach was a mess as she waited to hear the results. "The town wants you to stay. We want to help in any way possible. Evil has messed with the wrong town, the wrong townsfolk."

Zoey felt the tear slip from her eye as both humans and witches cheered. Lauren looked over at Slade, and with a motion of her eyes conveyed her thoughts. Walking side by side as the leaders of the Claritase and the Tenebris, Lauren and Slade parted the humans to walk to the stage and shake hands with Mr. Earnest.

"We're humbled and honored by your vote. For anyone with remaining questions, we will all be open to answering them for you. Do not hesitate to reach out to us," Lauren said with a smile.

"How will you know if we tell anyone about you?" a voice shouted from the crowd.

"Oh, we'll know," Slade said so confidently Zoey worried the deal might fall through right then and there. The fact was, they would only know by taking a peek into their minds. Specifically, the eight percent that voted against them.

"Slade," Lauren chuckled and some of the people laughed thinking it was a joke. "I will let you know that most of us will be traveling this day for healing. We will leave a group of witches here in case you need anything."

"How do we get a hold of you if we need something?" Fay asked from the crowd.

"It's the twenty-first century," Agnes called out. "Text us!"

A feeling of rightness settled over Zoey as her stomach and mind settled. They didn't need to run. But now it was time to make a stand.

4

Jane paced the kitchen floor as Galen worked up at the stones preparing them for the arrival of all the Moonshine Hollow witches. They'd spent all night looking through the diaries his Nan had taken pains to write over the centuries. There was nothing about hidden powers or taming an overflow of powers. Her body was humming with the full breadth of her powers and it was only because of Galen's healing touch that she was able to control them now. They'd assumed it was the bond of True Loves that allowed him to calm her after she'd accidentally grown a forest of tall trees behind the cottage when her powers had overflowed.

The knock on the door made Jane smile. It had to be Zoey. She knocked when no one else did. Jane ran across the room and flung the door open. She didn't bother to slow down as she hurled herself at the person who had knocked. "Zoey, I'm so glad you're here. I have to control my powers and need your help."

"Then you'd be better off asking us," Neferu said in her lofty manner from where she stood behind Zoey. Jane opened her eyes and saw Neferu gesturing to Agnes, Vilma, and Lauren. The grand mistress looked annoyed at having to be made to wait outside instead of just popping in and that made Jane laugh briefly. In that moment, no matter how put together Lauren looked, she had the glare of an annoyed cat on her face.

"Then please help me. I'll do anything," Jane said as she surprised Neferu by hugging her too. "Please. I feel as if I'm about to jump out of my skin."

Jane had inherited her mother's powers, which Aurora Kendrick should never have given Jane, but had done so to protect her. Jane's father, Anwir, was the head of the powerful Farrington family had wanted to steal them to enhance his own powers and to overtake the council. However, it wasn't just a little power between mother and daughter. Aurora Kendrick's powers had been illegally enhanced by Jane's grandmother's powers. Basically Jane was walking around with her natural powers plus two additional power sources—sources that were some of the strongest in Claritase and Tenebris history.

"Back to basics," Neferu said, storming into the room as if she owned it. "You forget all your witchling training."

"I never had any. My father wouldn't allow me to attend witch school," Jane admitted.

Neferu rolled her eyes. "If he weren't dead already, I'd kill him myself. Now, let's get started."

Jane glanced to the side as the rest of the council walked in carrying box after box and taking over her dining room table. Apparently the research to find a connection between them all was still ongoing. The prophecy had said, "*A traitor, a love taken, families destroyed all for power. A masquerade hiding evil has been in place too long. It's time to reveal who is under the mask. Only a power stronger than True Love can defeat the dark magic as evil as this. Only together can you stop it. Fate has played her last hand.*

Together referred to her, Galen, Zoey, Slade, Polly, and Samuel. Three True Love couples that were also best friends and now referred to as The Six. Jane's mother had appeared to her in a vision and had told her, "*The masquerade started long ago with each of you, but now you must work together to unmask the traitors. I gave you the power before you were born. You've had it all along. Your time to use it is now. Pull on the love that is even stronger than True Love. May the Goddess protect you and give you strength to do what I was unable to. To stand up against evil.*"

The council thought to find a connection between The Six to see if that would help determine the masquerade and who was behind the evil. Or at the very least, help them figure out how to defeat someone so powerful in the dark side of magic.

"Focus!" Neferu snapped, and Jane looked back at her teacher. "Now, let's get started."

All Slade wanted to do was focus on the case at hand—solving who was behind the dark magic. However, being the leader of the Tenebris was not helping him do that. Instead it was taking away from it. He had so many administrative tasks to see to with Lauren, it was driving him nuts.

"We need to focus on the case. Not giving our approval for marriages and all this paperwork. When did we get paperwork?" Slade complained.

"You're lucky it's paper and not stone tablets like previous grand masters had to use. Now, stop complaining," Lauren scolded.

They spent an hour working through petitions and

requests for assistance from witches all over the world. As they worked, Zoey, Polly, and Samuel went to the stones one at a time to be cleansed of black magic. Only after the work was done and the rest of the council was cleansed, did Lauren and Slade go.

Slade prayed to the Goddess and asked his mother and Linus for guidance as Galen scanned the warm glowing lights from the palms of his hands over Slade's body.

The warm light was soothing as he felt his powers basking in the energy. *Shared past.*

The words came to him suddenly and he blinked his eyes open. Galen lowered his hands and nodded. "You're all set. Is everything okay?"

"I heard something," Slade mumbled as he thought about the two simple words.

"Talk to your wife and Samuel and Polly. They both said they heard something too during the light therapy. Now," Galen said, rubbing his hands together, "I'm going to try a group session next. I'll be down at the house as soon as I can."

Slade felt free. He felt light and energized as he jogged past the long line of witches and down to the house. When he entered it he found the councils, minus Jane and Neferu, sitting around the living room. Papers and books were everywhere.

"Galen said you heard something during his light therapy," Slade said, cutting to the chase.

"We're waiting for Jane and Neferu. They're outside trying to see how Jane is doing at controlling her powers before we talk," Zoey said, holding out her hand for him. Slade walked over and instantly placed her hand in his.

"Your powers are flowing strongly," he whispered to her, but not quietly enough.

"So are Polly's," Samuel said, smiling down at his wife.

"We guys just can't compete," Slade joked as Zoey rolled her eyes at him.

"Okay," Jane said with a sigh as she joined them from the backyard. "I don't think I'll spontaneously combust anymore."

Neferu narrowed her eyes at her. "For now. You have a lot of basic self-control to learn. Has Galen cleansed your powers?"

Jane nodded and Neferu took a moment to cut the line to have Galen do his light therapy on her. Whatever power he had, it was like catnip to witches. It felt fantastic.

"Who heard things during your cleansing?" Slade asked, not waiting for Neferu to return.

"Wait, what?" Lauren asked. "You heard something?"

Slade nodded and noticed Zoey, Jane, Polly, and Samuel did as well.

"No one else did?" Slade asked the rest of the council who all shook their heads.

"Well, tell us what you heard, boy. Don't make us guess," Vilma scolded.

Slade had to smile at her but noticed it was once again the witch part of The Six who heard it. This was all coming back to them.

"I heard two words," Slade said slowly.

"*Shared past*," the five said together.

5

An irritated groan was the immediate response to their declaration. Slade looked questioningly over at Fern. "We've searched *everything*," Fern said with aggravation as she gestured to the boxes of records. "There is nothing in your past that would show The Six have any genetic link. Sometimes a few of you were in a room at the same time, but that's it."

The door opened and Neferu glided in, looking revived. Behind her, Galen stumbled in looking half dead.

Jane was up in a heartbeat and helping her husband inside. "Are you hurt?"

"No, love," Galen said as he fell onto the couch. "Worn out. I got impatient and decided to do a hundred witches at a time. I did it. They're great and back in Moonshine Hollow, but I kept hearing something over and over and knew I had to wrap up the cleansing and get back here. What does *shared past* mean?"

The entire group of six had been given the same message. Now, what did it mean?

"We can't find any shared past," Niles said since Fern

looked ready to tear out her hair.

"There is no shared past," Neferu said with certainty. "Galen and Zoey were born just decades ago, not centuries, thus negating any shared past with each other or others."

Zoey tightened her grip on Slade's hand as he looked down at his wife. Zoey's brow was furrowed and he could practically *see* the wheels turning in her head. It was the same look she had on her face when she had eyed the strippers' stage, trying to decide if she could rescue her client when they first met in Los Angeles.

"What is it?" Slade whispered to her. "Do you have an idea?"

"It's nothing," Zoey whispered back, but eavesdropping Lauren didn't agree.

"I think we need any ideas anyone has to offer. What has your mind turning, Zoey?" Lauren asked.

"It's actually something you said to the townspeople this morning. You were talking about witches and the powerful families to explain how witches have different power levels," Zoey said as Lauren nodded. "Could you repeat what you told the town?"

"Sure," Lauren said. "The strongest lines have been yours, Polly's, Jane's, and Slade's. Then of course Galen is the most powerful stone keeper."

"My father's line, Jane's mother's and father's line, Polly's mother's line, Galen's paternal line, and which line of Slade's?" Zoey asked. "After all, both his parents were grand masters."

"I can answer that. It was my mother's line. My father resented that. I think it's what drove him to break her down and eventually kill her. He wanted more power—power my mother had that he'd never get," Slade answered sadly.

"Same for me," Jane said, perking up. "That's not good

news, but it's a shared past."

"But that doesn't link me, Polly, or Samuel," Zoey frowned. "See why it's nothing?"

"It's not nothing," Fern said. She and Raiden were the genealogy experts and both were grabbing for books under piles of notes.

"Look," Raiden said as he pulled out the old tome. "The first Tenebris council was made up of a Farrington, Rode, and Katz."

"And the first Claritase council was Slade's mother's line, Habsburg, Polly's mother's line, Lurie, and Jane's mother's line, Kendrick," Fern said before looking up from the book. "Six total lines. Six total witches having a shared past."

Slade nodded understanding now. "Zoey is a Rode, I'm a Habsburg, Polly is a Lurie, Jane is both a Farrington and a Kendrick, and Galen is the grandson of the first stone keeper appointed by the Goddess herself."

"What about Katz?" Zoey asked.

"The direct Katz line died out at the uprising," Fern told her.

"Where do I fit in though?" Samuel asked. "I don't."

"Um," Raiden muttered as he flipped through a book. "You're a Mannering. It doesn't make sense. You're multiple generations from an original with no links to the other five."

"Blood doesn't lie," Galen said, moving to sit up. "Let me take everyone's blood, including my own. Maybe I can find something in it that links us."

"A Goddess gene or something," Zoey said with a nod. "It's worth a shot."

"This is very smart," Lauren said. "Linus had always wanted a blood tree. That's what he called it. Basically a genetic database of witches to track powers and strengths through the generations."

"Keep talking dirty to me," Galen laughed. "You've set my doctor's heart into an excited pitter-patter."

"You'd want to do that on top of being the stone keeper?" Lauren asked.

"I'd love to do it. I'll start right now. Give me your arms," Galen said, heading to the closet and pulling out his medical bag.

"Shared past or shared DNA?" Polly said with a shrug. "I guess it's all the same. I still think it's strange that it was Samuel and I who fought side by side at the uprising not even knowing each other. That's a shared past."

"My father killed your mother," Jane said apologetically to Polly. "Could that be considered a shared past between us?"

"That wasn't in the books," Fern said, looking over at Niles and Raiden.

"It wouldn't be," Niles answered. "Those two things are shared pasts, but not to the level of a marriage, child, or a union of some kind that were regularly recorded. Do any of you have any other links to each other like that?"

"Jane and I do," Galen said as he took blood from Samuel. "My grandmother wouldn't bless Jane's marriage to Ian. She warned Jane's dad there was a Selkie in the union and it would be cursed."

"A Selkie?" Niles asked, flipping through books excitedly.

"It's a Scottish story called The Legend of the Selkie. Scots believed there were seals that would shed their skin when on land to appear as human. If a human saw a Selkie without their skin, they would fall madly in love. However, it never ended well. All the stories ended in heartbreak. My Nan always taught me to take the warning of the story to heart–not everything in life is as it seems."

"The ultimate masquerade!" Jane gasped. Slade had to agree. But that wasn't the only masquerade.

"I also have something," Slade said, knowing as he said it was a shared past he should have seen before. "I'm the son of Helena Habsburg and Alexander Dohmen. My father took me from my mother and turned me into a Hunter. I was sent to kill Magnus Rode and his parents. Instead, I gave his parents a chance to hide him. I turned double agent to help the True Tenebris until it was no longer possible to do so."

"Wait!" Jane said, jumping as Galen tried to insert the needle into her arm. He gave her a look to calm down by wiggling the needle in front of her. "Sorry," she mouthed before turning back to everyone. "I see where you're going, Slade. Another masquerade."

"But not the last one," Zoey said, understanding where this was going. "My mother is human and what is that, but the ultimate way to hide my powers? Plus my father and mother hid both me and my powers until fate brought Slade into my life. However, the last connection . . . because Slade allowed my father to live, his actions allowed me to be born. I'm only here because of Slade's actions four hundred years ago."

"Obviously we know where my masquerade comes in," Jane said dryly. "Does this all connect back to Alexander?"

"What do you mean?" Lauren asked.

"Polly and Samuel met fighting Alexander. My father killed Polly's mother while fighting for Alexander. My betrothed was Alexander's second-in-command. Slade is Alexander's son and went against his father's orders to kill Magnus, thus allowing Zoey, his True Love to be born. That's five of us with ties back to Alexander and the uprising."

"We haven't reached the uprising yet in my Nan's journals," Galen said as he pulled the needle from Jane's arm.

"Which one is it?" Fern asked as she jumped up and faced the back wall.

"Um, there's five thousand of them," Galen said, nodding his head toward the giant bookcase taking up the entire length of the house and then some. "They're in chronological order. They're really fascinating if you can understand them. We couldn't figure out the historic way of recording information so we started with the most recent journal and are working our way backwards in time."

"I'd love to study them. The Library at Alexandria was one of my favorite places," Neferu said wistfully, walking over to the massive wall filled with a variety of journals. Some were on traditional paper, others not so traditional. "Five thousand years ago, when your Nan started as stone keeper, I was a young witch in Egypt."

"They begin there," Jane said, pointing to the farthest bookcase.

"So, we'll start looking around here," Niles said, plucking a book much closer to the end of the stone keeper's five thousand year reign than the beginning.

"1298," Niles muttered and set the journal gently back into the case.

"I've got 1436," Raiden said as everyone moved farther down.

"1523," Fern said. "We're getting closer."

"Let's start there," Niles said. "It's over a hundred years before the uprising, but we can see if she recorded anything leading up to it."

Jane jumped up suddenly and pointed at Slade. "Traitor!"

Slade hardly blinked. Why was she calling him a traitor?

"Jane," Zoey snapped. "My husband is not a traitor . . . wait, traitor!"

Slade glared at his wife who only smiled at him as Galen took his blood.

Zoey stood up too and grabbed Jane's hand as they practically bounced. "*A traitor, a love taken, families destroyed all for power*," they said together.

Zoey turned to him with a huge smile on her face. "Jane was right. This has to somehow go back to the uprising. Who was the biggest traitor of all? Alexander!"

"But, you killed Alexander, sweetness," Slade pointed out.

"I know, but it's part of the puzzle. He has to be the traitor."

"I could be the traitor. I betrayed my father," Slade told her. He didn't want to rain on her parade, but it wasn't clear yet. "Jane could be too. She betrayed her father by refusing to marry Ian, yet another traitor. However," Slade said, willing Galen to hurry up so he could pace as he thought, "my family was destroyed for power."

Jane bounced on the balls of her feet as she gripped Zoey's hands in hers. "Mine too!"

"Actually," Zoey said, stopping her bouncing, "I think you could say all our families were destroyed by Alexander's quest for power either because our families fought for Alexander or were killed by Alexander."

"Here's the uprising journal!" Raiden called out as the historians swarmed the books. "I think we need to look at it as a whole," Raiden said, turning back to the group. "The prophecy had said, *a traitor, a love taken, families destroyed all for power. A masquerade hiding evil has been in place too long. It's time to reveal who is under the mask. Only a power stronger than True Love can defeat the dark magic as evil as this. Only together can you stop it. Fate has played her last hand.* Then Jane's mother added; *the masquerade started long ago with each of you. Now you must work together to unmask the traitors. I gave you the power before you were born. You've had it all along. Your time to use it is now. Pull on the love that is even stronger than True Love. May the Goddess protect you and give you strength to do what I was unable to. To stand up against evil."*

"I think we've figured out our masquerades," Jane said.

"Not mine," Samuel responded quickly as Polly held his hand. "I'm the one who doesn't fit."

"We'll figure it out," Galen said with determination. "I need to get these to an actual lab to process."

"Leave us here with the books and we'll see what we can find," Neferu said. "We'll get you if anyone needs you at the stones."

"It's been a long day," Lauren said to the group. "Let's get home and get some sleep. We'll tackle this again in the morning."

Slade reached for Zoey and the second their hands clasped they were back in their bedroom in Moonshine Hollow.

"Slade?" Zoey said quietly as she took a seat on the end of the bed.

"Yes, sweetness?"

"Do you think I'll ever see my father again?"

Slade's heart broke for her. Zoey reached for him as her body was wracked with sobs. He pulled her into his chest and held her as she cried. She cried for the loss of her father and for the little girl who had spent her life thinking her father was dead only to have to relive it as a woman.

6

Zoey was quiet as she made her baked goods the next morning. Slade had undressed her and held her all night long after she'd cried herself to sleep. Zoey slept hard and deep, but that didn't mean she was well-rested. Instead, her mind had run a mile a minute with thoughts of her father. Could the family destroyed be hers?

She thought of her mother. Her mother still loved her father, but the love had turned from passion to friendship. Even Zoey's stepfather, Bradley, loved Magnus. Now Zoey was going to have to tell them her father was gone. Again.

The knock on the back door scared her more than if someone *poofed* into the kitchen. When Zoey answered it, she found Agnes and Vilma standing there. "We knocked. You happy?" Agnes asked as she pushed her way into the kitchen and tossed a treat to Chance. The black Labrador wagged his tail happily.

"Thank you," Zoey said with a forced smile.

"Come here, dear," Agnes ordered. Zoey stepped over to her and then she was in Agnes's arms with Vilma hugging her too. "We've got you, dearie."

Tarnation. The tears started again.

"You have a line a mile long on the sidewalk. Agnes and I will run the bakery this morning. You can stay back here or go home and rest," Vilma told her as she wiggled her fingers and the trays of muffins and other breakfast goodies floated into the display cases out front.

"Thanks. I'll just compose myself for a moment and then be out there to help you."

Zoey heard the door open and the front of the bakery fill with noise. Chance came up and nuzzled her leg. "I'll be okay, buddy," Zoey murmured to the dog she'd found by chance one night.

Zoey.

Zoey's hand froze on Chance's head.

"Dad?"

Zoey, help.

The voice seemed to be all around her as she leapt up from the stool. "I'm here, Dad. Where are you?"

Help me.

This time the voice came from one direction. Zoey's head whipped that way and she was running before she even registered the fact she was pushing her friends and townspeople out of her way. She shoved through them, ignoring all of their questions as she ran out of the front door of her bakery and into the street.

"Dad!" Zoey's tears came again as she saw her father staggering his way toward her. He was covered in blood and looked as if he hadn't slept in days. His clothing was torn and he was missing his shoes.

"Zoey," he said as she caught him. Her arms went around her father to steady him as the town filtered out onto the street.

"Oh my Goddess!" Agnes exclaimed as Chance growled at the scene.

"Wrong," Magnus hissed as a bolt of black magic shot from his hand and knocked Agnes back into the throng of people.

"Dad?" Zoey asked as her father began to laugh. "No," she cried as she pulled her powers forward. She knew that evil laugh.

"Give Daddy a hug." Evil enveloped her as the embodiment of her father wrapped her up in a hug. Tendrils of black magic shot from his hands into her back.

Zoey screamed in pain and arched back, trying to escape the pain she felt from the black magic wrapping around her heart, trying to rip her powers from her.

"Damn dog!" the impostor screamed, but Zoey was so lost she didn't see Chance biting the being. Instead, she focused her powers inward. She ordered her powers to her heart and felt the battle of good and evil internally. Her powers, a gift from the Goddess, attacked the black magic strangling the life from her as they tried to pull her powers from her body.

It was too late though. Zoey's knees gave out as her attacker laughed. A roar that Zoey felt deep in her being sounded as deep purple energy blasted the evil being. "Slade," she whispered.

Purple energy filled Main Street aimed right at the person or thing holding Zoey. Her powers sang, wanting to join in the battle, but Zoey was barely breathing. Her organs were shutting down and the last order she gave her powers was to fight for life.

. . .

Slade had felt the terror through their True Love bond. He'd transported instantly to the bakery only to find Agnes being flung through the air and hearing Zoey's screams.

"I can't stop him!" Vilma yelled as she used her powers in an all-out attack on the man holding Zoey.

"Magnus?" Slade gasped.

"It's not him. Save her!" Vilma said as she collapsed to her knees, blood streaming from her nose and ears.

Zoey screamed again and Slade lost all control. His powers surged free. He didn't hold them back as he shot them into his father-in-law. Slade stormed forward with a primal roar. Chance bit into Magnus again and violently shook his head as he tried to break Magnus's leg.

Slade's purple energy slammed into the figure that appeared to be Magnus, but was it? The being stumbled back, dropping his hold on Zoey. His True Love fell lifeless to the ground. Chance released his hold on Magnus's leg and went to stand between his mistress and the person trying to hurt her. The dog's teeth were bared as he barked and growled menacingly.

"Hello, my traitorous son." Slade watched as the figure turned from Magnus into Alexander before he turned the black energy onto Slade.

Slade's powers fought against it, but he wouldn't be able to hold it. He'd never felt such power before.

Alexander tossed back his head and laughed. "You're weak. You're pathetic. And now you're alone! Time to die."

Slade braced himself for the hit, but still stumbled back as the dark energy seemed to only increase in power. Slade could feel Zoey's life slipping away. He could feel the darkness closing in on her. The fear of losing his True Love sent his powers surging forward. He pushed the dark energy back with the love he had for Zoey, but he knew it was only a momentary victory.

"I'm glad I'll get the chance you kill you myself this time," Slade yelled at the figure who looked just like his father. The same father who killed so many of their kind for the greed of more power.

Power ripped forward from Slade's body. He yelled in anger, in pain from exerting so much energy and from fear. His father stumbled back and laughed.

"You're not strong enough. You couldn't take me on by yourself last time. Your woman had to beat me because you were too weak to do so. Doesn't look like she'll help you now. You're all alone," the figure now impersonating Alexander said with a smirk on his face.

"Wrong. He has us." Agnes's water power shot from her hands. Within a split second at least one hundred witches appeared in a tight circle around Alexander. Lauren issued commands like a general and Neferu demanded more from each witch. Samuel and Polly charged forward, wielding their powers like weapons.

Slade felt the dark magic falter and pushed his own powers to take the man down. Suddenly the dark magic flared and the man was gone, leaving behind only the echoes of his laughter.

"Zoey!" Maribelle yelled as she pushed through the witches to get to her friend.

Slade was already at her side. Their bond was weakening, but something wasn't right. He felt something pulling on his powers as if to rob him of his.

"I'm here," Lauren said, dropping to her knees and placing her hands over Zoey. Slade knew the answer just from the look on Lauren's face. "We don't have much time."

"Find Galen!" Slade ordered Samuel.

"Get out of the way or I'll whip you!" Doris Bleacher yelled as she pushed through the thick crowd. "Get her to the clinic. We can give her some oxygen until Doc Galen gets here," Doris ordered.

The cantankerous old secretary started making a path for them, but Slade didn't wait for that. He grabbed Zoey and, with a nod to Lauren, transported into the clinic. The lights were still off and the front door locked, but that didn't stop Lauren from moving into action.

"Use your True Love bond to keep her alive until Galen gets here. I can feel the dark magic around her heart," Lauren ordered.

"Well, aren't you zippy? What can I do?" Doris asked, seemingly annoyed they'd beaten her to the clinic.

"Get the oxygen and a shot of epinephrine. I don't know if human medicine will work on this, but just in case I want it on hand," Lauren told her, but Slade was already closing his eyes and drawing onto their bond.

Slade felt her powers struggling under the dark magic. The battle on the street was over, but the battle between good and evil was still raging inside Zoey. Slade put his hand over Zoey's heart. He closed his eyes and felt his hands warm. His powers were eager to answer the call for help coming from Zoey.

"Slade, it's me," Galen said softly as to not surprise him. "Keep doing what you're doing and I'm going to piggy back onto your powers to help Zoey. Just chant with me."

Slade felt warm hands cover his as a low, but strong chant in the old language began. Slade felt his powers surge to life. With his eyes closed, he could see the internal battle. He could see his powers joining Zoey's as they worked together to send the black magic into the nothingness her fifth element allowed.

Galen's powers fused with Zoey's and Slade's. It was like a spotlight shown onto Zoey's heart, burning up the dark magic. Suddenly Slade went stiff with a hit of new power. Galen's hands tightened around his as a lavender light, the same color as his and Zoey's True Love bond, hit Zoey's heart and exploded like a firework.

Galen's hand was ripped from Slade's. Galen was flung back as if he'd put his finger in an outlet. Slade's powers though didn't react the same. His powers encircled the lavender powers helping it focus on Zoey's heart. The darkness was gone and, with one more surge of power, Zoey's heart raced back to life. Her eyes shot open and her mouth dropped in a gasp.

"What was that?" Zoey asked as she placed her hand over Slade's above her heart.

Galen stood up from the floor. His hair was standing on end as he ran his fingers through it.

"I've never felt anything like that," Lauren said as if the power was still in the room and she didn't want to be hurt.

Galen cleared his throat. "About that. I found something in the blood. Let Zoey regain some strength and we'll meet when you're ready. I have some work to finish up and I'll present it to you then."

"What happened? Was that my father? Is he dead?" Zoey asked as Slade pulled her into his chest and held her. He was sure she could hear his racing heart, but he struggled to say anything. His love was alive. That was all that mattered to him.

"It wasn't Magnus, Zoey," Lauren said as kindly as she could. "It was evil. After you passed out, it took on the shape of Alexander and went after Slade. It was playing mind games with you."

Strong emotions rocked through Zoey and into Slade. "Then where is my father?"

"We'll find him, Zoey. I know we will. He hasn't come to us in any prophecies or visions so he has to still be alive." Slade tried to calm her but it wasn't working. He could feel her raw emotions racing through her.

"Do you think I'm dying?" Zoey asked. "Galen said he found something."

Slade didn't know what to do. Zoey was beginning to panic. Suddenly Doris, with her bejeweled cat's-eye glasses and gray hair pulled up into a bun so tight it pulled the wrinkles from her face, shoved her way into Zoey's face.

Slade put up a protective arm but Doris shot a glare at him. "Go ahead, leather boy. Give me a reason to spank you."

Zoey snorted out a laugh and Slade finally took a breath. It had become the worst kept secret in Moonshine Hollow that Doris liked to travel into the bigger town and moonlight at *specialty* clubs. The laugh changed everything though. Slade eased his grip on Zoey and let Doris get in close to Zoey.

"You're a strong woman. Sure, you're as nice and sweet as your treats, but you're also tough as nails. Are you really going to let that evil thing scare you?" Doris growled into Zoey's face.

"No," Zoey said softly.

"No?" Doris yelled back. "What kind of answer is that? That thing came in here and tried to kill you, tried to kill your love, and it threw Agnes across the street. Are you going to put up with that?"

"No!" Zoey said louder.

"No, what?" Doris growled, sounding every bit like a very strict dominatrix.

"No, *ma'am*!" Zoey yelled as she pulled herself free from Slade and stood up. Slade put out a steading hand to catch her as she wavered slightly, but she didn't need him right then. He felt her power surging back and he also felt the other power, the lavender one. "I'm going to learn what Galen found. I'm going to send that evil asshole into oblivion. And I'm going to find my father."

"Go get 'em," Doris ordered and before Slade could say anything Zoey *poofed* away.

Lauren's eyes were wide as she stared at Doris. "The Claritase could use you. Let me know if you want to become a drill sergeant," Lauren said before transporting away.

"You must be *very* popular at those clubs in Knoxville," Slade said with an impressed smile.

"In your dreams, leather boy," Doris said before walking out the door with what Slade could only describe as a hip-swaying strut.

Slade was still laughing when he transported and found Zoey and Lauren waiting for him.

7

Zoey was pumped. Doris's speech resonated in every inch of her body. Zoey was also pissed. She wasn't going to back down. No, she had the mother-Goddess fifth element. She was going to blast that evilness into nothingness.

"Zoey," Polly said, looking at her friend. "You're really shimmering. Like bright lavender unicorn-type shimmering."

"I'm worked up. I'm pissed. I almost died. That thing played with my emotions and . . . wait. You're shimmering, too." Zoey paused and looked at her friend. Yeah, unicorn sparkles summed up what was surrounding Polly.

"I guess the stones really got our powers recharged," Polly said with a shrug.

"Or could it be what Galen found in the blood?" Samuel asked. "Zoey had mentioned a Goddess gene. I thought it was silly, but maybe it's true?"

Neferu rolled her eyes. "There's no Goddess gene. We would have seen it before now."

"Then you tell us why they're shimmering like a sparkler?" Samuel shot back.

"I can do that," Galen said, appearing with Jane.

"Whoa, you're shimmering too," Zoey said to Jane. "More than the other day."

Jane smiled and nodded. "I think it's pretty."

"Galen, why are the women sparkling?" Slade asked, reaching out and taking Zoey's hand in his. Zoey instinctively leaned into him as they waited to hear what Galen found.

"First, is it okay to talk about your health reports with everyone here?" Galen asked. "I can talk to you individually if you prefer."

"I'm fine with now," Zoey said.

"Me too," Slade answered.

"We're family. We'll handle this together," Polly said as Samuel nodded.

Agnes and Vilma stepped forward to offer their support as well.

"Okay then." Galen pulled up something on his tablet and Zoey held her breath.

"You want the good news or the bad first?" Galen asked.

"Bad," everyone answered at once. Zoey was relieved. This anticipation was killing her.

"The bad news belongs to Samuel." Galen looked up from his tablet and then turned it around.

"Mine?" Samuel asked. His heart beat hard with fear. Was he dying? Was he infected with dark magic? He couldn't leave his True Love after finally marrying.

"The thing is," Galen said seriously, "your blood doesn't match up to who you say you are."

"Excuse me?" Samuel asked slowly. He didn't understand what Galen was saying.

"Who are your parents?" Galen asked, just as seriously.

"I already gave you that information," Raiden said, clearly just as confused as Samuel was feeling.

"What's going on?" Samuel felt anger building. Was Galen accusing him of lying about who he was?

"I don't know how to say this, but the people who raised you were not your biological parents," Galen said very professionally. He was in doctor mode, so much so Samuel was thrown by what he said. Galen delivered it as if telling him tomorrow was Saturday.

"Say that again," Samuel said and noticed Polly looked just as confused as he was.

"I pulled blood from the six of us, but also from the rest of the council. From my understanding, you are not related to anyone on the council, correct?" Galen asked.

"Correct," Samuel answered as Raiden nodded his agreement.

"That's not what the blood says," Galen said.

It felt as if Samuel's mind couldn't function. Nothing Galen was saying made sense. "That can't be right."

"I ran it twice and found your distant cousin and head of the Mannering family, Colin Mannering, to compare blood samples to. I'm sorry Samuel, but you're not a Mannering, biologically speaking."

"Then who am I?" Samuel asked, his body filling with dread and disbelief.

"You show a strong familial relationship to Agnes, Vilma, and Jane." Galen answered.

"Us?" Agnes and Vilma asked at the same time.

"*Me?*" Jane questioned with even more surprise.

"That's right. You three have a shared relative with Samuel," Galen told them.

Samuel shook his head. "No, that's wrong. Take my

blood again. I'm Samuel Mannering. Maybe one of my relatives is related to them and I got some of their DNA over the generations."

"Maybe from your maternal line. However, your cousin Colin is a Mannering. You two share zero matching DNA. Therefore it is impossible for you to be from the Mannering line. The amount of shared DNA you have with Agnes, Vilma, and Jane, shows closer familial relationship. Relationships like first cousins, aunt/uncle, great-aunt or uncle, niece/nephew, great-niece or nephew, half sibling, grandparent/grandchild, or great-grandparent are examples of the level of DNA you share. I'm hoping Raiden and Fern can help track down someone from your maternal line and let me take a blood sample. I also want to see all family that falls into those relationships to the three of them," Galen instructed Raiden and Fern who were already reaching for books filled with the genealogy of the Claritase and Tenebris.

Samuel just sat rigid as conversation flowed around him. His parents weren't his parents. Or, at the very least, his father wasn't his father. Was he adopted? Did his mother have an affair?

"They're still your parents," Polly whispered to him. "Even if you don't share DNA. They raised you, they loved you, and that's what matters."

Was that all that mattered? Samuel wasn't so sure. Whoever he was, there was a reason he was here and he needed to find out what it was.

Worried, Zoey looked over at Samuel. He looked miserable and she completely understood. She'd been excited when her father came back into her life, but she'd also felt betrayed. When there was a private moment, she'd have to pull Samuel aside to talk to him.

"If that's the bad news, then what is the good news?" Slade asked into the quiet.

She'd wanted to ask more questions, but instead Zoey kept her mouth closed as she waited to hear what Galen would say.

"When I ran your DNA, I found things that were clearly not human. I found the biological traits reflecting the strength and type of powers you have. What's really cool is in Jane's case. She had her inherited power trait, but was then gifted others' power. In humans, you can have two types of traits. Inherited and acquired. Inherited traits are in your DNA. You cannot change or alter your inherited trait. An example of an inherited trait is eye color. No matter what, on a biological level, you can't change your eye color because your DNA tells your body the color it is. That's inherited traits. That's what your powers are. Acquired traits are how you as a person develop as a result of external or environmental influence. These traits aren't in your DNA and can change over time, such as learning to swim or muscles getting bigger through weight lifting and diet."

Galen was practically bouncing with excitement. "It appears that witches are much more advanced than humans and have the ability to actually alter their DNA. It explains the True Love bond. Your eyes actually did, on a genetic level, change colors when you bonded to your True Loves. For Zoey, there's still the gene for your brown eyes, but there's now a new dominant gene for the lavender eyes you and Slade share. He is the same. The blue eye gene is now recessive and the lavender gene is dominant. Now, powers are different. There is no recessive or dominant. They're *all* dominant. So, when Jane's mother gave her the Kendrick powers, she literally gave her a piece of the Kendrick DNA that expresses as powers. It fused with Jane's power gene and now Jane has three genes, Jane's inherited one, her mother's, and the Kendrick gene from Jane's grandmother. All three are all working together as one gene."

"This is so cool," Lauren whispered with a teary smile. "Linus would have loved it."

Galen nodded. "It also appears that even when your True Love bond is broken, like yours, Grand Mistress Lauren, upon the death of your husband, you still maintain the genes from your bond. It's a way to stay connected."

Lauren placed a hand over her heart and smiled. Zoey had known Lauren had been married, but she never talked about her husband. However, her reaction to this news showed Zoey that Lauren still loved her late husband very much.

"That is very interesting," Slade said into the silence. "So are we supposed to give all our powers to us six and that's how we defeat the evil?"

"That I don't know. Jane's and Zoey's were the only ones I have fully sequenced so far. But this isn't all I learned from the blood," Galen said with a huge smile.

"Please tell me I can shape shift into a unicorn," Zoey pleaded with a smile.

Galen laughed and shook his head. "No, but your shape will shift. You, Jane, and Polly are all pregnant."

The room went dead quiet.

"I'm sorry, I don't think I heard that right," Zoey said slowly.

"The three of you are pregnant. Based on the hormone levels, Zoey, you're the furthest along at ten weeks. Jane is around eight weeks and Polly's is probably a wedding night baby. It's so soon for Polly it wouldn't show up in a urine test, but blood tests are much more accurate," Galen explained before turning to his wife to kiss her. "We're having a baby!"

"We're having a baby?" Zoey asked Slade who looked as close to fainting as she'd ever seen.

Samuel was in tears as he hugged Polly, but Slade just stared at Zoey. No one else made a sound, their mouths just hung open with surprise.

Zoey gently placed her hand over her stomach and closed her eyes. She focused all her power there. *Thump-thump-thump-thump.* Tears leaked from Zoey's closed eyes as she felt her baby's powers reaching out for her.

Zoey opened her eyes when she felt Slade's hands cup her still-flat stomach. He dropped to his knees in front of her, closed his eyes, and leaned forward to rest his forehead against.

"Hello, little one. I'm your father and I vow to protect you and your mother with my life. I vow to love you for eternity as I already love you more than I knew was possible."

Zoey gasped at the same time Slade did. Energy shot from the baby and sizzled along Zoey's skin to the point where it was like small static electric shock to Slade.

"The lavender power," Slade said suddenly before he kissed Zoey's stomach. "You saved your mother, didn't you? I felt you, sweetling."

She should be scared. She should be shocked. Instead, Zoey was filled with warmth and love.

Zoey looked up at the sound of sniffles. Lauren and Neferu were clutching each other as they cried happy tears.

"Little witchlings!" Lauren said with a huge smile.

"I can't wait to prepare the school. We must be ready for the new generation of Claritase and Tenebris," Neferu said as dabbed at her eyes.

"You all take tonight to celebrate," Lauren said, clasping her hands together. "We can continue this talk later. The team will be working on Samuel's past in the meantime."

"I'll have the rest of the DNA sequencing done as soon as I can," Galen told them all.

Slade lowered his head and placed his lips near Zoey's ears. "Let's go celebrate, sweetness."

Zoey grabbed her True Love's hand and left Scotland in a *poof*.

8

Jane looked down at her flat stomach and smiled. A baby. She was still in shock. She and Galen had celebrated privately in the small cottage behind their main house before Galen had snuck from bed to get Niles to transport him back to the lab.

The team was still in the main house reading everything they could find about the uprising and also tracing the family trees to find a connection between Samuel, herself, Agnes, and Vilma.

If Jane thought about it, she'd become consumed with the mystery of it. She'd want an answer right away as to how she and Samuel were related. She could do that in the morning. For tonight, she wanted to spend it with her and Galen's baby.

"Are you so sure it's Galen's?"

Fear shot through Jane as she placed a protective hand over her stomach and leapt from bed. "You're not real," she said, shaking her head at the man who had just spoken to her.

"I can assure you I am very real," the man said back as

he looked at her hands protectively covering her stomach and laughed. "You're so stupid. You always have been. It's why your father sold you to me."

"You're dead. You're not Ian. I watched the sad, pathetic, snotty man-child die. So, who are you?" Jane challenged the Ian lookalike.

"Ouch, love, that hurts," Ian said, grabbing his heart. "It doesn't hurt nearly as badly as what I'm going to do to you though."

"You can't do anything to me," Jane said, finding her voice. Ian had robbed it from her for four hundred years. She wasn't going to let him do so in death.

"That baby isn't Galen's." Ian leaned forward and dropped his voice. "It's mine and that baby is going to be just like his dad." Ian laughed and Jane fumed.

"I'm not the scared little girl I was centuries ago. I know you're not Ian. You're probably a magic spell or maybe you're the person behind all this business just having some fun. Whatever this is, whatever reason you're doing it, I don't care. You won't intimidate me. You won't scare me. You have *no* power over me."

"Aw, little Janey is becoming a big girl," Ian mocked. "Go ahead and tell yourself you're different. You can't change who you are. You're your mother's daughter–weak, pathetic, and useless," Ian spat.

"So weak and useless you wanted my powers?" Jane challenged. "Well, come and get them then."

Jane held open her arms as she stared the image of the man who had tormented her for centuries down. He laughed and then he lunged.

Jane stopped laughing when Ian's hands wrapped around her upper arms and squeezed hard. "See, the things from your nightmares are all true," Ian whispered with a laugh. A laugh that wasn't Ian's, but the same they'd heard with the dark magic. "Boo!"

Jane had to fight back the panic that was threatening her. This wasn't Ian. This was something else. Even dark magic had to be wielded by a person and she wasn't going to give into that fear. "Who are you?" Jane asked.

"I'm the person who is going to take everything from you."

Jane shook her head. "No, you're not. You're someone who must have been weak. In order to become strong, you turned to dark magic. You're nothing but a bully on a power trip. What happened to you that made you turn to the darkness?" Then it hit Jane. The prophecy was not just about The Six. It was also about whoever this was. "You're a traitor. Did you have a love taken or did you steal it for yourself when it wasn't returned? Did you destroy your family for power?"

The entity flinched and Jane pushed forward. "You've been hiding your evil side until Ian was killed. That was the first time we heard you. Did you love him? Is that it? Or was it Alexander who you loved?"

"You're the traitor. You all are," Ian spat. Darkness whirled like smoky tendrils around them.

Jane's time was up as the darkness curled like snakes about to strike. Jane could stay and fight or *poof* away. The prophecy said it took The Six of them. She hated to do it, but as the tendrils lunged at her, Jane *poofed* to the main house.

"He's here!" Jane yelled as the researchers looked up with surprise. "He tried to trap me in the cottage."

Neferu sent a text, and within seconds The Six and the entire council were back in her living room.

"What's going on?" Zoey asked as they all looked around the room waiting for him to pop out of the shadows.

"Ian appeared to me," Jane said as she filled them in. Galen held her as she talked. Jane felt his powers searching her body for injuries and didn't stop him. "Is the baby safe?" she asked when she'd finished telling them about her conversation with Ian.

"Yes. You left before the dark magic could enter you."

"I hated running," Jane said with a frown.

"It was the right thing to do," Zoey told her with a kind smile. "We'll do this together."

"We need to move this to Moonshine Hollow," Slade told them. "That way we'll all be close by."

"Galen," Neferu said, turning to Jane and Galen. "Can we box up all these journals and bring them to Moonshine Hollow?"

"Of course," Galen said.

"I'll go pack," Jane told the group. It was time to go back to Moonshine Hollow and face evil head on.

9

Samuel said goodnight to Slade and began his nightly walk through downtown Moonshine Hollow. It had been three days since they'd returned from Scotland. He was on edge waiting for another attack, but all had been quiet.

"Hi Samuel!" a group of Irises called out as they headed to their club. Samuel waved and hurried across the street to open the door to their meeting area.

"Thank you," Fay said with a wink.

"Such a nice young man," Peach said with a smile.

"I heard you're going to be a father. Is that true?" Ada asked, causing a pileup at the door.

"Polly's pregnant?" Peach asked so loudly that the entire Iris membership heard and were crowding the door faster than he imagined so many hip and knee replacements could move.

"She is," Samuel said with a big smile. He was still so proud and excited about becoming a father that he would happily discuss it for hours.

"I think," Ada said, raising her voice for the entire group

to hear, "that Polly isn't the only one pregnant. I saw Jane and Zoey looking at a baby site this morning."

"They could be looking for Polly," Fay pointed out.

Ada shook her head. "Not when they were setting up their own accounts."

All heads turned as one to Samuel.

"How on earth could you see that?" Samuel asked, trying to get the off topic. It wasn't his place to share news of the other couples' pregnancies.

"I saw them through the window of the bakery with my binoculars. I was doing my community service of witch watch. We've started a volunteer group to keep our eyes out for that bad witch," Ada said as if it made perfect sense.

Samuel had learned one thing while living there almost a year. He knew when to skedaddle, as Peach would say, and this was one of those times. "Ladies, it's been a pleasure. I have to get home and see how Polly's doing."

Samuel could have walked off, but they'd catch him. Some of those old ladies had scooters. So he took advantage of them knowing about witching and *poofed* back home. He'd do a walk through town later after the Irises were done with their latest true crime documentary.

"Samuel?" Polly asked, coming into the living room from the small kitchen. "What are you doing here so early?"

"The Irises were interrogating me on Zoey's and Jane's pregnancies. I am a mighty warrior. I have faced down the worst evil in history but those old ladies terrify me," Samuel admitted.

"There, there. I'll protect you from those scary senior citizens." Polly thought she was being cute. She thought he was joking, but just wait until the Irises cornered her. Then she'd learn the truth of his statement.

"Did you hear me?" Polly asked, pulling Samuel from his thoughts.

Samuel pulled her into his lap and placed one hand over their baby. "Sorry, love. What were you saying?"

"She was saying we are on our way over," Lauren said. Only centuries of training kept Samuel from jumping at the voice behind him.

"We?" Samuel asked before placing a kiss on his wife's cheek. She looked worried and he wanted to fix that.

"Yes, we," Neferu's stern voice answered.

Samuel turned around and saw it wasn't just Neferu and Lauren. The entire council was there, including Fern and Raiden, the heads of genealogy. "Did something happen?" Samuel asked as he prepared to fight evil once again.

"We don't know. We were just summoned here," Slade said with a shrug as he kept a protective arm around Zoey.

Agnes and Vilma nodded too. They didn't know why they were summoned either. Samuel held Polly's hand in his as he prepared to go to battle. "You found out who is behind the dark magic," Samuel stated.

Fern shook her head. "No, but we found out who you are."

Samuel felt Fern's words like a hit to the chest. He physically recoiled, causing Polly to reach up with her other hand to grip his upper arm to steady him. "I'm Samuel Mannering."

Fern looked ready to wilt under his sharp tone. "I'm sorry, Samuel, but biologically, you're not."

"Then who am I?" Samuel growled, sending the genealogist a couple steps back.

Raiden, the Tenebris genealogist, narrowed his eyes at

Samuel in warning. "We're trying to help you. Don't be a jerk to us for doing our jobs."

Samuel let out a long breath. He wasn't like this. He protected the innocent, not yelled at them. "I'm sorry, Fern. My whole world is about to be turned upside down."

"Not your whole world," Polly whispered to him. "I'm still here and so is your little witchling. No matter what you learn, you have a family who loves you."

Samuel placed a kiss on Polly's cheek and then faced the researchers. "Okay. Who am I?"

Fern took a deep breath and began. "Raiden and I have gone back through the family tree and circled anyone related to Jane and to Agnes and Vilma. Then Niles and Neferu went through the Claritase and Tenebris records the two years leading up to your birth and the two years following your birth. This is what we've found."

Samuel leaned closer to the paper she was holding up and saw a ton of names listed. Was he related to all of them?

"There are so many," Samuel said and Fern nodded. "This is your paternal line. Then Galen worked on the DNA sequencing more to mark it down as shared paternal or maternal lines. That led us to this."

Fern pointed to the list and everyone went silent. They stared at the red circle and no one breathed.

"Are we all reading that right?" Jane asked what he wanted to ask.

"That can't be right. I've never met that person before. Ever," Samuel said, not computing what he was seeing.

"It doesn't matter if you never met. Your biological mother did," Raiden said as gently as possible.

"I'm a Farrington?" Samuel said with disbelief.

"Not just a Farrington, but *the* Farrington. As the last surviving male of the line, you're the head of the Tenebris

Farrington family," Raiden told him even as Samuel was turning to face Jane.

"You're my little sister?" Samuel asked the face that mirrored his own shock.

"Half-sister, but yes, she is," Galen confirmed.

Tears welled in Jane's eyes and then she was throwing herself at him. Samuel caught her instinctively and felt great heaving sobs coming from her body. Galen looked ready to kill him. Polly was crying. Oh Goddess, everyone was crying. Samuel felt a tear roll down his face and buried his head in his sister's neck. He had a little sister.

"I have a big brother," Jane said between sniffles as she tried to stop the tears.

"I'm Samuel Farrington?" Samuel asked again as reality was slowly sinking in. He hadn't been the head of the Mannering family. That was his distant cousin, Colin. But he had always been a Mannering and now he was a Farrington. Not just that, but the last male in an original line and head of the family.

"Wait a second. Let me get this straight," Zoey said, taking a deep breath. "Slade is the head of the Habsburg family. Polly is head of the Lurie family, and Jane is the head of the Kendrick family. Those are the original Claritase families. Then Samuel, since he's older than Jane, is the head of the Farrington family, and my father is head of the Rode family. But we don't have a head of the Katz family?"

"Sweetness," Slade said quietly. "There's a possibility you're the head of the Rode family."

Samuel saw Zoey recoil at the thought. "No. He's still alive. He has to be."

"At the very least Zoey is the heir to the Rode family," Galen said gently. Everyone was aware Zoey was close to breaking over the fate of her father. "But, we found a direct Katz heir."

"What?" Lauren practically shouted. Samuel let go of Jane and turned to the shocked grand mistress who hardly ever lost her composure like this.

"This is trickier," Neferu said to the group.

Raiden stepped forward again. "Let us talk you through this. We started with Agnes and Vilma's relatives since the DNA results showed a small amount of common DNA. We shared this list of possible relations with Galen," Raiden held up pages and pages of people Agnes and Vilma were related to.

"How could you narrow it down?" Samuel asked.

"It's all science. DNA doesn't lie," Galen answered. "I went around and got samples from anyone who was still living. From that, I was able to narrow down if you were related to Agnes and Vilma through their maternal or paternal line."

"Katz," Samuel heard Agnes whisper to Vilma. He wanted to ask them about it, but Raiden was talking.

"With that information we were able to cut the list in half," Raiden said, turning to Galen have him pick up the story.

"It's a long process but the general gist of it is I can tell your approximate relation based on the percentage of shared DNA. The person Samuel shares the most DNA with was a granddaughter to the original Katz line who is still alive. Her name is Isla. However it wasn't a direct lineage connection. We found the common ancestor you all share with the help of genealogy and DNA. The one whom Samuel, Isla, Agnes, and Vilma all share the DNA from."

Fern held up a family tree and Samuel leaned forward to read it.

"Who is Merhotep?" Samuel asked as he looked at the chart.

"Oh my Goddess," Lauren gasped. "She was the first-born daughter to the original Katz family. To understand this, you must read the history books. The six council members were created by the Goddess and gifted with a True Love. The True Loves had no surname and no special powers. They had regular powers, but not strong enough to detract from the leadership of the six members. The Goddess also created other witches with less powerful powers to help populate— well, that's another story. They were all to be a support for the original six. When Merhotep Katz was born, she inherited a lot of her father's incredible power. The Katz line is no longer an active line because the direct line never continued as the direct heirs didn't have children. It was diluted as it branched farther and farther away from the direct line. As far as I know, there are no direct heirs of the original Katz family."

"But Agnes and Vilma are related to the Katz family," Samuel pointed out. "So the line isn't dead."

"Yes, dear. But we stopped having witchlings before the uprising and sadly none are alive today," Vilma answered kindly.

"The last Katz who could have furthered the line was a woman on the Claritase council named Lizbet. Alexander killed her at the uprising," Lauren explained.

"Not just her, but he killed the entire future of the Katz line. Lizbet was pregnant when she was killed," Neferu said with a frown. Merhotep was my friend and mentor. I was that to her descendent, Lizbet. Lizbet believed she was carrying a boy and was planning on petitioning the council to name her son as the head of the Katz family."

"You can do that?" Samuel asked.

Neferu nodded. "If you are a direct heir, you can revive the line. Prove the lineage and you can revive the old family name and the power that comes with it."

"Lizbet knew she was pregnant with a boy," Lauren said sadly. "She was so excited to have the six originals families back in leadership roles. She believed it was her calling. That was the plan when the Goddess first created us. The six families would lead, acting much like a council, with grand mistresses and grand masters elected. However, then witchlings came along and not all Tenebris had male heirs or Claritase female heirs so the council became more of a general council."

"So Merhotep isn't my mother?" Samuel asked.

"Merhotep had two daughters. Khepri was the oldest and most powerful, like her mother. Then Sanura was the youngest," Fern explained.

"Yes," Agnes said with a nod of her head. "Sanura was our grandmother. Are you saying Sanura is Samuel's relation?"

"Relation, yes." Galen paused and pulled up something on his tablet. Samuel waited impatiently as Galen tapped the screen. "Here is Agnes's DNA and here is Isla's. She's Sanura's youngest daughter and is still living. Like Agnes and Vilma, she is past the age to have witchlings. You see the strong DNA resemblance?"

Samuel nodded. There were lots of matches.

"Here is Samuel's, Isla's, and Agnes's." Galen held up the screen again. "The highlighted marks are the matches. The amount of matched DNA shows that you have more in common with Isla than with Agnes, but not enough to be a direct relation. Sanura can't be Samuel's mother, but someone very closely related to Sanura has to be."

"Are you saying what I think you're saying?" Lauren asked slowly.

Galen nodded. "I think Khepri is Samuel's mother."

"That's not possible. Khepri didn't have children. She never married. She inherited more power than Sanura and had dedicated her life to the council," Lauren said, surprised.

"I agree with Lauren," Neferu added. "I knew Khepri very well. She was never with a man. I've been telling you this," she said to Niles, Fern, and Raiden.

"This is where we disagree," Niles told them. "We went off of Galen's hunch and followed Khepri's records on the council. She took a leave of absence to visit her sister before her untimely death."

"I remember that. I was new to the council but she went to stay with her sister," Lauren said slowly. "She died suddenly, by accident. She was gathering food when a Hunter accidentally shot her with a bow."

"No," Agnes and Vilma said at the same time.

"We regularly visited our grandmother back then and Khepri was never there," Vilma told the room. "Grandmother Sanura was pregnant with her last child then so we helped with the delivery."

"She was a grandmother and pregnant?" Zoey asked with surprise.

"Witches don't age like humans," Agnes reminded her. "And it was her last child. It was Isla."

"Then where was Khepri?" Samuel asked.

"That's what we're still working on," Niles said. "What makes me think she is your mother is the fact her date of death is listed as the same day you were born."

"Who reported her death?" Lauren asked.

"Her sister," Niles answered. "Whatever was going on, Sanura was a part of it."

"Are you saying there's a possibility I'm also now the head of the Katz family?" Samuel asked slowly as he tried to wrap his head around generations of DNA and forensic genealogy.

"That's exactly what we're saying," Raiden answered.

10

Zoey was so busy during the morning rush that she couldn't catch her breath. The townspeople learning about witches hadn't harmed her business. In fact, it had only gotten busier. She found that the witches wanted homemade pastries, while the magically-made treats fascinated the humans.

The rush was winding down when Slade walked in. She'd found that a member of the Tenebris warrior group usually spent the morning in the bakery pretending to be chatting or eating breakfast. Zoey knew better. Her True Love was protecting her when he couldn't be there himself.

"How are my girls?" Slade asked as he leaned over the counter and kissed her.

"Girls?" Ada asked from across the room. She must have special witch hearing because there was no way a human could pick that up. "Does that mean Zoey is pregnant and with a girl?"

Zoey shrugged and looked at Slade. "You started it."

She hadn't wanted to tell anyone until she'd found her

father. Zoey didn't know why, but every feeling she had said he was still alive.

Slade smiled mischievously at Ada. "I'm putting in the practice, Ada. I promise."

"Then who are the girls?" Ada asked, sure she'd trapped him there.

Slade's smile grew wolfish as he glanced at Zoey's chest and then back to Ada with a wink. "My favorite girls."

Ada huffed in defeat and the rest of the people went back to eating and talking.

"I felt you this morning," Slade whispered. "Did you pick up on your father?"

Zoey shook her head. "If he's still alive, he's nowhere near Moonshine Hollow."

"We'll find him," Slade promised.

"So, now you think I'm having a girl?" Zoey whispered.

"I always thought you would." Slade leaned forward and kissed her again. If only they could enjoy this moment, but it wasn't meant to be. Screams echoed through downtown. Slade was already out the door before Zoey even made it around the counter.

"What in tarnation?" Ada asked as she came to stand next to Zoey on the sidewalk.

Main Street was filled with the cutest little critters—fawns, squirrels, chipmunks, and bunnies. The trouble was those critters were chasing around the witches and trying to kill them.

"Zoey!" Slade yelled a second before an adorable bunny with floppy ears and a wiggling pink nose barred its teeth and leapt for Zoey's throat.

A ball of fire energy slammed into the bunny, saving Zoey. When Zoey looked for the bunny, it was gone.

"They're just chasing the witches," Ada said as she

slammed a squirrel trying to attack Zoey's leg with her massive purse. "Geez Louise, did they pick the wrong town. Everyone here has a hunting license by the time they're ten."

Doors up and down the street were flung open. The sound of rifles being loaded echoed off the street. The high school rifle team marched into position at the end of Main Street. With a series of whistles and arm movements, the residents of Moonshine Hollow lined up on one side of the street. They stood almost shoulder-to-shoulder as the coach for the rifle team and avid hunter, Stan Bartly, held up his arm. "Witches, run to us!"

Maribelle's husband, Dale, shoved Zoey behind him, aimed his rifle and waited. Ada and the Irises kept the cute killer critters back with their purses, rolling pins, and brooms.

"Transport!" Slade yelled.

"We can't," Polly said from where she punted a chipmunk that then just vanished.

"Run. Now, now, now!" Stan yelled. He was in jeans and a polo shirt that was embroidered with Moonshine Hollow Rifle Team on the pocket. He was in his late forties and stood tall and in charge next to his students.

Zoey reached for Polly as Fay smacked a fawn on the head with her rolling pin. "Why are they vanishing?"

"They're not real," Zoey said as it dawned on her that these were magically created animals versus real ones. "They're like the snakes! They'll bite but when they're dead their power leaves them."

"Ow! They can still bite!" Eileen screamed as blood poured from a bite on her leg. She turned and zapped the squirrel into nothingness.

"Let me see," Galen called out as he ran toward them from the clinic. "Black magic! Try to not get bitten."

"Aim," Stan's booming voice echoed. "Fire!"

Woodland critters *poofed* from existence all around them like bubble gum bubbles being popped. Black tendrils of dark magic floated up into the air where the cute critters had been.

"Well, darn," Billy Ray said as he stroked his long gray beard. "I had a hankerin' for rabbit stew, but none of them were real. It was like we were playing a video game."

Zoey nodded as she looked onto a completely empty Main Street. It was as if nothing had happened.

"Get it out!" Eileen said between clenched teeth. Zoey looked back at her and found her lying on the ground with Galen's hands blazing bright as he covered the wound with them. "It hurts so badly!"

Galen began to chant, his hands grew brighter, and then there was the release of the dark magic into the air from Eileen's bite.

"They might not have been real, but they could do real damage to witches." Galen stood up and looked down the road at all the witches huddled there. "Is anyone else bitten? If you are, you need to speak up. The bites infect you with black magic," he yelled.

A few hands shot up and Doris was there before Zoey and Galen. She was organizing witches into triage based on the damage of the bite.

"I think I'm going to have to change my opinion of Doris," Zoey said to Polly, who could only nod absently in response.

Polly's forehead creased and she leaned forward as if trying to see something. "Is Billy Ray's beard moving?"

Zoey looked up at the Opossum's bartender. His gray beard did look like it was moving.

"Billy Ray!" Zoey called out as she took off running towards him.

"Yes, Miss Z?"

"Your beard!" Zoey warned. The closer she got the more movement there was in his lumberjack-sized beard.

Billy Ray reached up and ran his hand over it before jerking his hand back. "Dang! Something bit me!"

"Snakes! Your beard has gone full Medusa!" Zoey yelled as she joined him.

Bart, the doorkeeper of the Opossums, reached up and felt his beard. He too gave a bellow of surprise when his beard hissed at him.

Otis turned and looked into the large glass window of the storefront behind him and screamed like a twelve-year-old girl. It didn't matter each of the men were over sixty-five. They were in a full-blown meltdown as their beards writhed and slithered on their faces.

"I got you, honey!" Peach screamed as she ran toward her husband, Otis. In one hand was a rolling pin. In her other her hand was a large kitchen knife.

Considering most of the men in town had some sort of beard, utter and complete chaos erupted as their beards turned into snakes.

Peach had a little smile on her face as she hacked the snakes off her husband's face with the knife and then beat them with her rolling pin until they went up in black smoke.

"Bart, cut out your caterwauling," Fay admonished as she grabbed the hunting knife clipped to his belt and sliced the snakes away. Ada waited until they fell and then smashed them with her purse.

Zoey rubbed her hands together and held them up to Billy Ray's face. She kept them out of the snapping range of the snakes as she let loose a ball of white energy. She directed it to cover Billy Ray's beard as the big burley bartender looked ready to pass out from fear. "Hold steady," Zoey told him until the snakes were fully engulfed in the white light. Then she flicked her fingers and the snakes disappeared into nothingness.

"Use control!" Lauren yelled to the witches lining up to help the men. "If you can't control your power, let someone else do it."

"You can lose control with me," Justin Merkle said with a wink to Phoebe. The sweet witch was new to Moonshine Hollow and Justin had been flirting with her since they first met in Zoey's bakery. Justin had always run on the rough side of life, but he'd changed his ways three months ago. It just so happened he changed them the day he met the air witch.

The cute blonde witch blushed. Her eyes were the lightest shade of blue and they twinkled whenever she was around Justin. B.P.—before Phoebe—Justin had been a shaggy dog. His hair looked as if he'd never cut it nor brushed it. He usually just shoved it under a ball cap. He had no real occupation. Instead, he worked odds jobs. After meeting Phoebe he cleaned up his act and his clothes. He opened his own home repair and painting company and was busier than he could have hoped.

"Aw, Justin's growing up," Dale muttered, and Zoey smiled as she worked on the snakes on Dale's face.

She was happy for Justin, and she was happy for Phoebe. Phoebe was quiet, but a very competent witch. She'd make the perfect witchling teacher. The idea slammed into Zoey as she placed her hand over her baby.

"There, no more beard," Phoebe said with a little smile to Justin as the snakes blew away.

His hands flew to his face. "My beard is gone!"

"Forty-three years of marriage and *finally* it's gone!" Peach laughed as her husband's hands flew to his face. "The evil witch thought she was hurting us, but we've been wanting our men clean shaven for decades."

"No!" Otis and the rest of the Moonshine Hollow men cried in despair.

"I think you look handsome without a beard," Phoebe told Justin.

Zoey dropped her hands from Dale's face. "It's nice. They're all getting along. I'm happy for Phoebe and Justin. Next!"

Dale walked off and his friend Ethan stepped up in line. Zoey cringed at the copperhead snakes the redhead had in place of his beard. "Miss Z?" Ethan asked. "Do you think Ember would care if I'm not a witch?"

Zoey glanced to where the fire witch was helping remove the snakes from one of the old men who belonged to the Opossum club.

"I don't think so," Zoey said as she focused her power on the copperhead beard. "Why didn't you go to her for help?"

"I'm too nervous, Miss Z. I mean, look at her. She's so beautiful. What would she want with a country boy like me?"

"Trust me, she'll find a lot to like, Ethan." All six and a half feet of a man built like an action hero with the heart of a teddy bear. "Hey, Ember!" Zoey called and the big man in front of her clammed up. "Can you help me with Ethan here. I think it might be a redhead thing. These copperheads don't like me."

"Sure thing," Ember smiled as she blasted the last of the snakes off the elderly man's face. The fiery redhead walked over and suddenly looked a little shy. "I've been wondering what you'd look like without a beard. I'm excited to see it."

"You've been thinking of me?" Ethan blurted out and then pulled himself up to his full height with pride. "I've been thinking about you too."

Zoey stepped back and took a look at downtown as Slade joined her. "Whoever did this thought to divide the town. They didn't. They brought the town together." Zoey watched as single witches and humans talked, laughed, and flirted. She watched as Fay, Ada, Peach, Agnes, Vilma, and the rest of the Irises played matchmaker for witches and humans alike.

"The town has never been so united," Slade said in wonder as he slid his arm around her waist. "Well, except for them."

Zoey turned to see a group of men and women huddled together staring daggers at everyone. They were the ones who had voted against the witches. Clara, who had been a friend, was whispering to a large man she recognized as one of Dale's friends. She couldn't remember his name, but it was clear he didn't agree with Dale's take on witches.

"You think they'll keep our secrets?" Zoey asked.

"I don't know, but I'll talk to Samuel tomorrow. We need to keep an eye on them."

11

Slade found Samuel at the sheriff's office early the next morning. There had never been so many couples out on first dates as there were last night. The diner had been packed to capacity and you could feel the love in the air.

However, Samuel wasn't smiling. Instead, he was staring blankly at the computer.

"You okay?" Slade asked.

"I'm confused to say the least. How can I be the head of both the Farrington *and* Katz lines?"

Slade let out a sigh. He and Zoey had talked about it last night as they lay in bed. He'd placed his hand over her abdomen and radiated his love for the new life nestled there. Although, Zoey thought it was a boy, he was sure it was a girl. "I think this is about setting things to rights. The original six were supposed to be good leaders and instead, there were cases of betrayal. It's up to the last in their lines to fix it. Zoey and I also realized this next generation would be able to start over with a clean slate. Our children will lead the original six families with no treason, with no lying, and with no hiding. It'll be a new start, a rebirth, of the Claritase and Tenebris."

"This whole thing has nothing to do with the six of us, personally, but with something that started centuries ago as a power grab. It all goes back to Alexander. I've been thinking about it all night. But Alexander wasn't one of the original six council members."

"He wanted the power of them though," Slade said about his father—a father he wished he never had. And the kind of father he swore he'd never become to his little witchlings.

Samuel let out a sigh. "I wish I knew more about who my mother was, how Anwir Farrington became my father, and why I was raised as a Mannering."

Samuel paused just as Slade did. "Do you feel that?" Slade asked, shooting up from his chair.

"Fear," Samuel said as he similarly was up and out of his chair.

Witches were in a panic and their fear could be felt through the earth and on the wind. Slade threw open the door and ran toward Zoey's bakery. He couldn't see what was going on through the crowd of people, but he knew the smell and saw the smoke. A witch had been burnt.

Zoey's bakery was full as Doris's perpetually annoyed face came to the counter. "I thought you were a witch and all magical."

"Um, I am," Zoey said, not knowing where Doris was going with this.

"Then why are you burning your muffins?"

"I don't have any muffins in the oven," Zoey said a

moment before a wave of fear hit at the same time the screaming started.

"Fire!" Maribelle yelled.

The bakery emptied out and Zoey froze at the sight in front of her. A pyre was set up with wood around it. A witch was tied to it and fire consumed her, nearly in an instant. Zoey couldn't see who it was as Agnes let loose with her water power to squelch the fire at the same time as other water witches moved into action. They weren't alone. Maribelle and other humans shoved past with fire extinguishers in hand. Off in the distance, the sounds of the lone fire engine roared to life. It was too late, though. The witch couldn't be saved. The black smoke curled into the air and Zoey felt it like a punch to the gut as the smoke formed letters. *You're next.*

Zoey felt the fear shoot through her body as she began to tremble. A witch had been burned right on Main Street and they hadn't been able to save her. She was too far gone by the time anyone was alerted.

Zoey smelled the burnt flesh, smelled the ash, and smelled the dark magic. It was rotten and foul and smelled like the death it had just delivered. Through the chaos, Zoey heard the screams of terror. Heard the tears of pain. Heard the laughter of evil.

"Sweetness!" Slade was by her side with his arm wrapped around her. "It's okay, breathe."

It was then Zoey realized she was shaking. Not from fear as she had thought, but from anger so deep she felt it in her soul. She felt a darkness in her heart unlike anything she'd ever felt before. She wanted revenge. She wanted death. She wanted utter destruction.

The unity that was created last night was gone. Witches pulled away from the humans to form a huddle on one side of the street. They looked fearfully at the humans as talk of leaving Moonshine Hollow to hide was whispered about.

Justin walked forward from the crowd of humans. He walked across the street and straight to Phoebe. "Phoebe, I fell in love with you the first time I saw you smile. You made me the person I am today with your goodness and your kindness. You didn't laugh at me when I was at my lowest. You helped me up and gave me purpose. I'll fight to protect you from whoever or whatever did that. I am lucky to have you in my life. I love you, Phoebe."

Tears streamed down Phoebe's cheeks as her friends held her protectively as if Justin might set her on fire at any minute. "Oh Justin, I love you too!"

Phoebe broke from her friends and threw herself into Justin's arms. The anger Zoey had felt vanished as love filled every fiber of her being. Humans and witches met in the middle of the street to hug. Some to even kiss like Justin and Phoebe and Ethan and Ember. Others hugged each other tightly. The entire Iris group wrapped Agnes and Vilma in a protective group hug. This wasn't dividing them. This was showing true friendship.

"Love will always win, right?" Zoey asked her True Love as she placed her hand over their baby.

She looked up at Slade as he bent to kiss her. "Always, sweetness."

Zoey felt something deep inside her unlock. She felt as if a part of her hidden away had opened up, letting a flood of energy loose in her body.

"You're glowing, sweetness," Slade said as he stepped back from her. "Like, really glowing."

"Oh my Goddess," Vilma whispered as all talking stopped. The entire town turned to look at her and took a giant step back.

Zoey held up her hands but couldn't see them through the white light. Her powers were coming to the surface, moving, swirling, and growing. Zoey was filled with it—love. Love for her husband, love for her friends, love for her town, and love for her baby. She couldn't contain the feeling that was overwhelming her in the best possible way as she looked at the people she loved.

Zoey placed her hand over her still-flat belly and watched with wonder as a lavender light began to glow and swirl with hers. Through the brightness of her powers, Zoey saw Slade's hand cover hers. A mix of power, of energy, of magic swirled around them in white, lavender, blue, and red until the entire town and all the witches standing on Main Street were awash in it.

"We're not leaving," Zoey said, although even to herself her voice sounded different. It sounded sure, authoritative, and divine. "Love and friendship is the ultimate way to defeat evil. Together, we'll defeat evil."

12

Polly clasped her hand with Samuel's as they walked down Main Street behind the urn Grand Mistress Lauren carried. The witch who had been killed was named Luna. She was a young witch, born right before the uprising, from an inconsequential line. She had minimal powers and wouldn't have stood a chance at defending herself against evil this strong.

The town had insisted on joining the funeral in accordance with Claritase tradition.

As a group, they walked down Main Street and into Earnest Park. Luna was an air witch and as such would be released back to her element.

Polly sniffled as they clasped hands and formed two rows of semicircles with Lauren and Slade in the middle.

Lauren took off the top to the urn and held it up into the air. "We give you thanks for the time we had with Luna. Earth to earth, water to water, fire to fire, air to air. You graced us with your powers and we give back to you our Luna. May she be blessed by the Goddess forever."

As one, all the air witches broke from the lines and

stepped forward. They held up their hands and let their light blue air power free. It circled the urn, reaching inside, and then with the color of the air and the burst of the wind, Luna was returned to the Goddess.

Quietly, everyone turned to leave. Polly rested her head against Samuel's shoulder as they walked solemnly from the park.

"The council needs to meet at Zoey and Slade's. We've found the answers."

Polly's head jerked up at Neferu's words. Polly looked up at her husband and saw his jaw clench. Samuel had been a bundle of nerves the past week. She'd felt him adrift and tried to be his anchor. The time was finally here. He'd have his answers and it would be up to her to hold him together as his world broke apart. Nothing he'd known was true and Samuel was having a hard time reconciling that.

"We'll meet you there," Polly responded for both of them.

Samuel waited for Neferu to leave before speaking. "How am I to hear my mother and father weren't my parents?"

Polly stopped and pulled on his arm to bring him to a stop beside her. "They *were* your parents. They simply didn't contribute any genetics to you. They raised you, they loved you, and they made you the man you are today."

Samuel nodded, but she could tell he was upset. "Let's find out what happened and how I came to be."

"You're here for a reason, Samuel. We all are. It's not how you came into the world that matters. It's what you do when you're in it."

. . .

It's what you do when you're in it. Samuel froze at the impact of her words. He turned and placed a hard kiss on Polly's lips.

"As always you bring me back to what's important. With you by my side, I can face anything."

When he kissed his wife again he transported them to Zoey and Slade's house. The living room was already full with the council and the researchers. Samuel's heart pounded nervously as he waited to hear how things centuries ago played out to make him the man he was today. "You've found something?"

Niles and Neferu stood up with a book lying on the table between them. "We have. It's the missing puzzle piece," Neferu said before looking toward Niles.

The Tenebris researcher cleared his throat and picked up a book. "Alexander Dohmen was not from a powerful Tenebris line. However, he never let that stop him in his bid to become grand master. In order to do so, he needed to kill the previous grand master and take control of the council. We actually found the answers to what happened hundreds of years before the uprising."

"Where did you find these answers?" Samuel asked.

"The stone keeper's journals. We found the time you were born and went backward. There we found a young Alexander coming to the stone keeper for help because he wanted to grow stronger. The story is easier to follow if we start there," Niles said before turning to Neferu and giving her a nod.

"Three hundred years before the uprising, Alexander Dohmen came to the stone keeper to ask the Goddess to bless a marriage—a marriage, according to the stone keeper, to Khepri Katz," Neferu told him.

"What happened?" It was Slade who asked this and not

Samuel, but he wanted to know just as badly. "Because we know my father didn't sire Samuel."

"No, he didn't. The stone keeper denied the match. Merhotep made her disapproval well known, as did the stone keeper. Alexander Dohmen wasn't powerful enough for her daughter," Neferu answered. "So Alexander married Helena Habsburg three months later. He lied and told her the Goddess and the stone keeper blessed the union. It wasn't blessed by either of them."

"In the meantime, Merhotep and her father were desperate for a male heir to carry on the Katz line," Niles said, picking up the story. Merhotep brought her eldest daughter, Khepri, to the stone keeper. Galen's Nan wrote that darkness cloaked Khepri. No happy ending was in her fate. Her fate was sealed and only Khepri could stop the darkness to come. She warned Khepri to never marry and to never have a witchling, as that child would be an instrument of evil."

Samuel felt as if he'd been punched in the heart. He was that child. He was that instrument of evil.

Niles looked at him steadily and continued. "Two hundred years before the uprising, Anwir Farrington came to the stone keeper with a dilemma. The Farrington line depended on him siring a male heir. He wanted to keep the line powerful, and while Aurora Kendrick was willing to marry him, he also had his eye on Khepri Katz and the elusive Katz line."

"Your Nan told him Khepri was not for him. That Khepri was never to marry," Neferu said as she handed Samuel one of the stone keeper's journals. "Read it."

Samuel looked down to where she pointed. "I knew the darkness I'd seen when Merhotep Katz had brought her eldest daughter to me was going to break free and there was nothing I could do about it. I warned Anwir Farrington from Khepri Katz. She was much older than him, for one thing. I tried to steer him in the direction of another, but he wouldn't have it. It was either a Katz or a Kendrick and both brought centuries of despair. The youngest Katz was already married and producing female heirs aplenty. Still, not a single male heir to take the Katz power and lead the Tenebris line," Samuel read.

"Continue reading," Neferu said quietly.

Samuel took a deep breath and looked back down at the journal. "Anwir Farrington had a darkness in him much deeper than Alexander. He argued with me and said that because he was The Farrington he could take any Claritase he wanted. I warned him against such a thing. I tried to scare him. However, he left my house determined to take what I had told him was not available. His last words echoed in my heart and soul. He laughed when I told him Khepri wasn't for him. He said he had a Kendrick already, but he'd take a Katz, too, if he chose, and there was nothing anyone could do to stop him."

Samuel closed the journal and handed it back to Neferu as Jane came forward and wrapped her hand around his. His sister was here to support him for they shared a horrible father. A father with ties to evil.

"There's more," Niles said into the silence.

"Read it," Samuel ordered. He didn't think he'd be able to form the words right now.

Niles picked up another journal. "The next year," Niles said and began to read. "Khepri Katz showed up at the cottage tonight. Tears streaked her face with shame as her sister, Sanura, helped her inside. I asked her what ailed her."

Niles cleared his throat and took a deep breath before

continuing. "What Khepri told me was the realization of the nightmares I'd had since Alexander left my cottage. Khepri told me that Anwir Farrington tried to court her, but she'd taken my warning to heart. She'd turned him down. Anwir left angry. His sister, Loralei Farrington, had come to speak with her to see why Khepri had turned her brother down. Khepri told Loralei about her meeting with me, and the warning I had given her. Because of that warning, Khepri hadn't married her love, Alexander, and she'd hated to break his heart. Loralei told her she didn't need to worry as Alexander was well loved now. Now she needed to focus on love with Anwir."

Niles looked up from the journal. "Are you sure you want me to continue to read? I can give this to you and Jane to read in private."

Samuel shook his head. He needed to hear it all. "Go on. What else did Galen's Nan write?"

Niles looked back down at the journal and continued to read. "Loralei Farrington insisted Khepri accept her brother's marriage proposal. The Farringtons and Katz lines combined would be even more powerful than any others on the councils. When she refused, Loralei threatened Khepri and it ended with Khepri using her powers to make Loralei leave. Two nights later Anwir Farrington and his sister, Loralei, abducted Khepri from her dwelling. Anwir pleaded with her, told her he loved her, told her he'd do anything to be with her. Khepri tells me she felt as if she didn't have control over her body or mind. She agreed to marry Anwir even though she knew it was wrong and not what she wanted."

"She was possessed?" Polly asked.

Neferu nodded. "We know it's possible for witches to possess humans, but it's very rare for witches to be able to possess other witches, especially someone as powerful as Khepri. I'm guessing she was drugged, to weaken her powers and resistance, then with her walls down, possessed. That's how she can remember everything, but also knew it wasn't her making the decisions. Humans don't remember any of it. But someone as powerful as Khepri? She'd have fought against it."

"What happened next?" Jane asked Niles.

Niles cleared his throat and looked back down at the journal. "They were married in a secret ceremony, but one that was never registered with the council, and therefore invalid. Khepri told me of a wedding night she'd never consented to, but was powerless to stop. The next morning she awoke and she had the ability to control her mind and body again. Anwir wasn't in the room and she heard voices. She slid out of bed and followed the sound. She found Alexander, Anwir, and Loralei in the kitchen talking."

"The deed is done. A Farrington male will be born to a Katz combining the two powers into one child that we can control," Loralei Farrington laughed as she lifted a goblet up in celebration.

"You are brilliant for a woman. You set up every detail of this plan," Alexander said, saluting Loralei before kissing her passionately on the lips. *"A Farrington and a Katz witchling. My wife is with child and soon I will control the heir to the Habsburg line too. As soon as I get the brat, you and I will be able to be together forever. We'll be the heads of a dynasty for millennia to come."*

"To our children ruling the world," Anwir said, holding up his pint.

"A world where humans serve us!" Loralei laughed as the three of them toasted.

Samuel felt Jane shaking next to him and wrapped his

arm around her as Galen rubbed her back. "It's okay. They're gone now. They can't hurt us any longer," Samuel said to his sister.

"My father and aunt were behind the uprising."

"Don't forget he was my father too," Slade said with his jaw tight and his hands fisted in anger.

"But what happened to poor Khepri?" Polly asked.

Niles turned the page in the journal and began to read. "Khepri escaped and made her way to her sister before telling her all of what had happened. Together they decided to pretend nothing had occurred with Anwir Farrington. Khepri was on the council and she'd stay surrounded by friends and family to prevent Farrington or his sister from reaching her again. The wedding hadn't been legitimate, and since there was no evidence of it, she decided to hide in plain sight. Until she began to show that she was with child. They came to me tonight and I felt the babe. He was strong and evil hadn't touched him yet.

"You must tell all that Khepri is ill and staying with you. They won't come after her then. We'll deliver this babe here at the stones with the presence of the Goddess," I told the Katz sisters. "Now we wait."

Niles looked up from the book and Samuel knew what had happened even before Niles went back to reading. "The stone keeper talked about other witches who visited the stones and how for almost four months your mother lived with her and her husband at this cottage. She was hidden here and safe. She was happy. The stone keeper writes, *"I have never seen such a love for a babe as I do when I watch Khepri through her pregnancy. She sits in the stones and sings to him every day. Every moment she tells her babe that he is loved and that he is blessed by the Goddess."*

Samuel closed his eyes. He would have sworn he felt a

light touch on his shoulder, but when he turned, no one was there. "How did I end up with the Mannerings?"

"That's coming up next," Neferu told him. "Go on, Niles."

"Khepri's son will be born any moment," Niles read. "An answer from the Goddess herself came today. A lovely couple, Ellis and Catherine Mannering, visited and prayed for a child. They have been unable to conceive and begged the Goddess for a miracle. Khepri walked to the stones where they were crying and simply reached down and took their hands in hers. She placed them on her belly as a contraction rippled through her. *'This is your gift from the Goddess. You must never tell anyone where you got him. His life and his soul are in danger. Promise me you'll love him and raise him as your own,'* Khepri said to the young couple."

Niles looked up and caught Samuel's eye. "You were born that night with the Mannerings holding your mother's hand. Her last words were a plea for your safety." Niles looked back down at the journal and read, "A boy was born. Light, not darkness, shone upon him from the Goddess herself as tears flowed in the stones. The life was draining from Khepri as her sister held her in her arms. Khepri looked to the Mannerings as she kissed her son on his head. *"Please name him Samuel. I will guard him from the heavens as you guard him from here. The Goddess has spoken and she has told me he will be a mighty warrior. Allow him to train as one day he'll save us all."*

"Khepri kissed her son one last time, whispered some words in the babe's ear, and held her hand over his heart before she went to meet the Goddess," Niles finished reading.

The room was silent except for sniffles and a few sobs.

Samuel stared at the closed book Niles held out to him. It was his story. It was his calling. It was his purpose.

"We believe your mother passed on all the Katz power to you before she died. Galen confirmed it in your DNA," Neferu said quietly. "In this room we have the councils, the original six council member families, and the stone keeper represented. Claim your name, Samuel."

Samuel felt it in his heart. He may be *the* Farrington, but that wasn't who he really was. He wasn't Anwir Farrington's son. He was Khepri Katz's son and he was the Mannerings' son.

"I ask that both the Claritase Council and the Tenebris Council name me Samuel Mannering Katz, only son of Khepri Katz and Catherine and Ellis Mannering. I also petition the council to put an end to the treasonous Farrington line, once and for all." He felt Jane stiffen beside him. "If my sister so agrees. Otherwise, I relinquish all claim to the Farrington name and her son can claim it."

"My son will be the stone keeper and my daughter will be the Kendrick. I believe the punishment of stripping the Farrington name of all power and rights is a just one for the treason they committed. When we die, the Farrington line will die with us." Jane reached over and took his hand in hers. The stood united as they faced the council.

"I feel we need the approval of the Goddess. Let's go to the stones to deliberate. We will meet you there in thirty minutes," Lauren said with the full majesty of her position as grand mistress.

13

Samuel arrived in the circle after thirty minutes of strolling the countryside to find the council still sequestered in the cottage for further debate. Taking advantage of the quiet, Samuel stood in the center of the stones as the councils discussed his request. The questions of his history had been answered and now plans for the future were to be made. He'd been out of sorts since discovering he wasn't a Mannering until now. Now he stood in the circle and opened his powers to the Goddess and to his mother.

"I thank you for your gift, Mother Khepri. I won't waste it. You and Mother Catherine would love my wife, Polly. We're going to have a baby. The Katz and Lurie lines will continue with all the goodness and love we have."

Love surrounded him and he could feel the magic of the stones resonating around him.

"Samuel," Polly called softly from the edge of the stones. "They're ready for you and Jane."

"I should have asked you before I petitioned the council," Samuel said as he laced his fingers with Polly's.

"The Farrington name is a powerful one. You might want our child to have it."

"Oh, Samuel. Don't you know by now I never cared what your name was or what line you're from. I care that you love me, that you are kind, and that you are honorable."

"Thank you, Polly. I love you."

"I love you too. Now, let's find out what I call you," Polly said with a wink.

Lauren and Slade stood in front of the council. Jane stood next to Samuel as they faced them and waited to hear the result of the vote.

"Upon reviewing the evidence for ourselves," Lauren said with authority, "the Claritase Council hereby revokes the Farrington name and lineage from all future records and posthumously holds Loralei Farrington guilty of treason and guilty for the abduction of Khepri Katz. The council approves to change Jane Farrington's name to Jane Kendrick as evidenced by her Kendrick powers that were passed down to her, overriding her Farrington powers."

"Similarly," Slade said as the acting grand master, "the Tenebris finds Anwir Farrington guilty of kidnapping, rape, and treason. The Tenebris Council hereby revokes the right for any person to claim the Farrington name after today. Further, the Farringtons' seat on the council is hereby revoked. With evidence that Samuel Mannering was in fact born to Khepri Katz, the Tenebris council hereby revives the Katz family line. May the Katz line live long, proud, and honorably from this day forward."

Samuel took a deep breath but then jumped forward as Niles and Neferu prepared to write the order into the official history books for the Tenebris and Claritase. "Stop!"

"What are you doing?" Neferu demanded. "It has to be recorded so all members will be notified of the update."

"Wait, give me a second. Whoever has embraced the dark magic knew we were in Moonshine Hollow. They've been tormenting us there, but before that they had sent Ian and possibly Alexander. If we write this in the books, there is a good chance they will see it and know we're making the connections of the past to better understand our future. If they see we're catching on to them, they could run before we find out who it is."

"Samuel's right. Write it down, but not in the books. We'll enter it later," Slade ordered Niles who quickly closed the official history book.

Neferu looked to Lauren who nodded in agreement. Samuel breathed out a sign of relief. He felt whole again. He'd always been confident in himself and the love his parents had for him, but now he felt more rounded. The strong powers he possessed, why he was a warrior . . . it all made sense now.

"Do you ever feel your mother touch you?" Samuel asked Slade a couple minutes later as everyone talked in the cottage before heading back to Moonshine Hollow. Galen was writing down the notes from the meeting into the stone keeper's journal. He'd started to pick up where his Nan left off. As soon as they were done, they'd head back to Tennessee. "I mean, it sounds stupid. Pretend I didn't ask that."

"It's not stupid," Slade finally said. "I have felt her giving me power, leading me in the right direction. I'm sure both Khepri and Catherine are working together to help you."

Slade looked as if he wanted to say more, but he stopped as his brow creased. "Is that Zoey?"

Samuel looked out the window. Zoey walked stiffly up

the path toward the stones. While that wasn't alarming, the bright glow coming off her was.

"Something isn't right. She doesn't walk like that," Slade muttered one second before leaping across the couch and flinging open the door to run after her.

Zoey.

Zoey had been standing back, watching as her friends accepted and embraced who they truly were when she'd heard her name called. She'd turned her head toward the stones and saw him. Her father. As if she were transfixed, she walked out the door and straight toward him.

Zoey. Help me. You're the only one who can save me.

Zoey slowed her fast footfalls as the memory of evil masquerading as her father slammed into her. However, her feet didn't stop. They couldn't stop.

She felt her powers reaching out to him. Saw the white light of her power expanding through space and time to protect him.

"Dad?" she asked as she approached the figure in the circle tentatively. "How do I know it's you?"

"*You're my Jellybean. I don't have much time. I'm using all my power to get this message to you.*" Zoey nodded as she joined her father in the circle. "*Take my hand so you can see what I see.*"

"Zoey! Stop!" she heard Slade yell from behind her.

"*I'm sorry, Jellybean, but it has to be now or never.*"

Zoey slowly reached out her hand to his. He appeared as nothing more than a shimmering figure, but when her hand reached for his she felt it. "Dad!" she said on a gasp as their powers sang in recognition.

Zoey felt her head snap back as the circle in Scotland

disappeared. She couldn't hear Slade or even feel the cool Scottish air. Instead, she was in an old stone room that reminded her of a castle that had seen better days.

"See what I see."

Zoey had no control as her father moved his head slowly up and down and from side to side. Chains, anchored to the walls, were clamped onto her father's wrists and ankles. Tapestries like none she'd ever seen before hung on the wall. One was a crest of some sort and her father spent a long time staring at it.

"I don't know who took me. I know so few people since I was born after the uprising. He's powerful, though. He's blocking my ability to transport and every few hours he comes in here to try to steal my powers. I'm almost drained, but I've been hiding some until I could gather enough to reach you. I don't have much time left, Jellybean. He wants you. He wants you all."

"I'll save you, Dad," Zoey yelled as she fought to keep her grip on her father's hand as the heavy lock tumbled. The door opened slowly and she saw a booted foot enter the room before her father blinked and she was back in Scotland with Slade gripping her arms and shaking her.

"Come back to me, Zoey!" Slade yelled as everyone hovered around her. The entire council and The Six were all together in the stones looking worried.

"I need to see the coat of arms for every family," Zoey said so suddenly and decisively that she surprised Slade.

He paused for a moment, and then pulled her to his chest in a tight hug. "I thought I lost you, sweetness."

"Never going to happen, but I know where my father is. He showed me the room he's being held in. There was a tapestry with a crest on it," Zoey said into his chest as her heart beat rapidly. Time was running out and she had to save her father.

"Tell us about the crest," Fern ordered as she and Raiden pushed their way forward.

"It was a red and gray shield. There was a roaring gold lion head on the top, then in the two red quarter panels of the shield there was a silver snake twisted into a circle. On the silver quarter panels there were—"

"Black daggers with ruby hilts?" Jane asked, her face completely blank of emotion.

"Yes," Zoey said slowly as she turned to Jane. "You know it?"

Jane nodded. "It's the Farrington family crest. The black dagger with the ruby is part of the Tenebris symbol. Lion stands for strength. The circular snake ouroboros is a symbol of eternal life. A tapestry with that crest used to hang in Farrington Castle."

"Where is Farrington Castle? Could my father be held there?" Zoey asked as the feeling of time running out started to weigh heavily on her.

"It's in the English countryside. The middle of nowhere actually. I haven't been since I was a little witchling. I honestly didn't think it would still be standing," Jane said.

"We need to go, right now," Zoey said. She felt it from the roots of her hair to the tips of her toes. Her father was about to die. "Shoot. Dad said he couldn't transport. Someone was blocking it."

"But who is there? We're the last Farringtons," Jane said as she motioned to Samuel.

"Maybe, maybe not. You never know who else Anwir forced himself on," Slade pointed out.

"Could whoever this is be using black magic? Could they be the one behind all of this?" Slade asked.

"We all need to go together. We can only defeat whoever

it is if we act together," Zoey said as Niles ran up with an ancient looking map.

"Here's the estate. Here's the nearest town we could transport to." Niles pointed to the map and then looked up.

"How do we get to the castle?" Zoey asked.

"The old fashioned way. We drive," Niles answered.

"Let's go get my father back and put an end to this dark magic once and for all." Zoey looked around the stones at her friends. They were risking their lives for Magnus and she didn't know how to repay them. However, there was no flicker of doubt or hesitation.

Zoey held out her hands. Slade took one and Jane took the other. Soon they all stood in a circle holding hands. With a swift prayer to the Goddess they were on their way to rescue her father.

14

It had taken longer than Zoey liked to get to Farrington Castle. The property has been fenced off with large signs promising dire punishment for any trespassers. The fields surrounding the castle were overgrown and the gravel lane was practically washed away. The large metal gate guarding the property was sturdy and the lock on it was new.

"We can just pop over to the other side," Zoey said as they stared at the tall fence and gate.

"Wait," Galen ordered as he cocked her head and looked around the property. "I feel dark magic. It's all around. It extends from the ground up and probably encloses the entire property. If you use your magic, whoever set the protection spell will know you're here."

"Won't they already know with you doing your stone keeper thing?" Zoey asked, her patience running out.

"No. That's like comparing apples to oranges. This protection is to keep other apples out. I'm not even on their radar."

"So, how do we get in if we can't use our magic?" Jane asked. She looked pale as she stared off into the distance.

"The old-fashioned way," Slade answered. "We scale it."

"Maybe when I was a thousand years old I could do that, but until you open the gate, there's no way I can get in," Agnes told them with a shake of her head.

"Do we have to scale it or can we knock some of it down?" Zoey asked Galen who shrugged as if to say he didn't know.

"If it's a traditional protection spell to keep out other witches, it won't pick up if a non-witch enters," Lauren said, looking back to Galen. "I bet you're pretty strong. Want to try to kick out some of the fence so we can get through without magic?"

"Keeping breathing, sweetness. We'll be in soon," Slade whispered in her ear sensing she was about to explode with impatience.

Galen looked around and then looked back at the van. "Give me all your belts," Galen ordered as he raced back to the van. He grabbed the keys from Niles and was backing it up toward the chain link fence as belts were collected.

"Just the leather ones," Galen said as he got out of the van. He plucked four from the pile and looped them together. The first one in the leather belt rope looped over the trailer hitch on the back of the van. The last one in the rope looped through the wire fence. "There."

Galen got into the van and slowly pressed on the gas. The fence groaned, but held its ground. Galen pushed down on the gas, giving the van more power to pull. The tires spun, the engine revved, and then the van shot forward, dragging a section of the fence behind.

Zoey should have waited, but the second the fence was out of the way, she was running toward the castle. She bent low and hid in the tall grass until she got closer. It was then she saw the castle wasn't rundown at all. It looked to be in perfect condition. The lawn surrounding it was pristine. Flower beds and picture-perfect gardens surrounded the house.

"Was there a window?" Slade whispered in her ear as his hand closed around her arm to prevent her from running forward.

"What?"

"In the vision. Was there a window?"

Zoey thought back and nodded. "Yes."

"Then he won't be in the basement. Anything else you can tell us so we can narrow down his location?"

"It was a smaller room. One window. It has a small fireplace, but nothing was burning. The room was square shaped."

Slade looked up at the castle. "He's not in the turrets or any of the larger rooms that you'll find on the first or second floors."

"Rafters!" Zoey suddenly remembered. The ceiling was made of rafters. Not plaster."

Slade kissed her quickly. "He's on the top floor. Break up into groups. Try to find access points where you can enter with no magic. Galen, you walk around to help the groups enter the house.

"Jane, Polly, and I should be a team," Samuel said, reaching out for his sister.

Slade nodded. "You find whoever this Farrington is. Search the main floor first going in through the front door. Remember, you have the advantage. They don't know who you are."

"Fern, Raiden, and Lauren take the right side and search the second floor. Zoey, Agnes, and I will look specifically for Magnus on the fourth floor and will enter through the back door. Niles, Neferu, and Vilma, take the left side and try to get to the third floor," Slade ordered. The grand mistress didn't even blink at being commanded. It was clear Slade was the one with the plan.

"I have the special juice," Agnes said, patting her fanny pack. "I've been carrying it since Magnus went missing."

"Quiet and don't use magic unless you absolutely have to," Slade said before going silent.

Slade reached back and took Zoey's hand in his and had her reach back for Agnes. Like a snake they weaved silently through the tall grass until they approached the back door. They kept low and ran across the trimmed lawn until they reached the door. Zoey waited as Slade reached up and slowly turned the old lock to the door.

The sound seemed to echo in the night air and Slade froze. They all waited and listened for any movement inside. When none came they snuck in. They were in the old kitchen of the castle. Zoey felt as if she were stepping back in time, although the kitchen had been updated with modern appliances and lighting.

Worn stone flooring met their feet as they walked silently inside. They walked by a massive kitchen island with a butcher block top and into a room with a long-benched table.

"That's the servants' staircase," Slade whispered as he nodded to the dark narrow stairs. Even with lighting it still looked gloomy. "They'd take the food up that way to the main dining room."

Slade took the lead as they climbed upward. Four flights up they came to a door at the top of the stairs. Everyone leaned against the cold stone and listened.

Zoey wanted to call for her father to tell him she was coming, but she couldn't risk blowing their cover.

"Control yourself, dear. Save it for when you need it,"

Agnes whispered. Zoey was about to ask what she was talking about when she noticed her hands were glowing again.

Zoey took some deep breaths and focused on pulling her energy to the tips of her fingers, just underneath the skin. Her powers churned impatiently waiting for release as Slade slowly opened the door.

The hall was long and narrow. To the left was a door and to the right was another door. "Those will lead to the men's and women's servants' quarters," Slade said, pointing to the doors.

"It's all a kind of power play," Agnes said. "If this Farrington is old school, he'd put Magnus in the men's quarters so Magnus understands he's nothing more than a servant to Farrington. However, since there's a window, it was a coveted room. On the men's side that would belong to the head butler."

"Which way?" Zoey asked, her powers desperate to escape to go look for her father.

"Let's try left first. It's closer to the front door. There may be another servants' entrance for the footmen and butler to answer the door," Agnes answered.

They followed Slade in a line as their feet fell on worn wooden planks in the dark and damp hallway. Slade reached out and turned the knob. The door didn't open. He put his ear to the door and gently knocked. A second later the faint sound of metal tapping metal could be heard.

"This is the right door," Slade whispered. "Stand back."

Zoey took a step back as Slade kicked his booted foot near the locked doorknob. The door splintered and crashed inward.

"We need to hurry. They'll have heard that," Slade called

out as he was already running through the door and into the servant's hall.

"First door on the right," Agnes called out as they entered the men's servants' hall. She was hot on Zoey's heels and already had the thermos of her magic rejuvenation drink in her hand.

"Locked," Slade said with annoyance. He didn't have to tell them to back up this time. Zoey and Agnes were already in position on each side of the door.

"Kick it down and I'll go in blasting to protect you if Farrington is in there," Zoey told him. She saw he wanted to protect her, but instead he trusted her to protect him. He gave a curt nod and as he kicked the door in, she brought her powers up into her hands.

The door flew inward and Zoey jumped in front of Slade with her powers ready to take a hit, but none came.

"Dad!"

"Jellybean," he smiled, but he was so weak it only came out as a whisper. "He took the last of my powers I didn't hide. I used the rest to keep him away from my special powers. The Goddess came to me while I was chained here. The special blue powers, she told me I have to save them to help you. They're a gift of her love for us. The fate of our kind depends on it. But it's not me helping you. You're the one helping me now."

Zoey clutched her father into a tight hug. Relief at seeing her father alive hit her so hard tears rolled down her cheeks as she hugged him.

"We're family. We help each other." Zoey kissed her father's cheek as she tried to stop her tears.

"I've got you, Magnus," Agnes said, dropping to her knees and shoving the drink into his mouth. Magnus drank it down like a man starved.

"I can't get the chains," Slade answered. "I'll have to use my powers. If they don't know we're here yet they'll know now."

Zoey held her father against her chest afraid of what would happen if she let him go as he drank Agnes's drink. "Do it."

Slade melted the chains from Magnus's arms first. He would have fallen over but Zoey caught him and held him to her. In short work he was free. "See if you can transport," Slade told Agnes.

"No. They must not have found whoever this Farrington is yet," Agnes responded.

Zoey's heart dropped. They had to get her father to safety. The magical smoothie was kicking in, but her father was in no shape to fight. He looked as if he'd aged centuries.

"It's not whoever. It's The Farrington," Magnus muttered.

"We know it's a Farrington," Agnes said, but Slade cut her off.

"Zoey, Agnes, take the lead. Go to the end of the hall. I saw an open doorway. That must lead to the front door," Slade ordered them as he bent down and lifted her father into his arms. "I know you'd prefer to walk out, sir, but this is the fastest way to get everyone to safety."

Zoey's powers were itching to be let free. The anger she felt toward the person who did this to her father threatened to overtake her.

"If you need to, leave me behind. Save them," she heard her father tell Slade.

"I'm sorry, sir. I can't do that."

"Why not?" Magnus asked his son-in-law.

"Because our witchling isn't going to grow up without a grandpa. Now be quiet and let's move."

Zoey could feel the love and happiness her father was exuding. She wouldn't allow darkness to rule her. She was better than Farrington. She had love on her side.

15

Jane found the front door unlocked and took the lead as they entered the castle. She remembered the layout although the castle had changed a lot in four hundred years. She noticed electric lights and modern décor mixed in with the antiques within the stone walls.

Jane saw light from the fireplace flicker under a closed door as they made their way down the hall. She motioned for Samuel and Polly to stay by the door. She needed to do this first part herself. It was her family name after all. Jane didn't knock, she just opened the door and strode in as if she still lived there.

Her father, whom she thought long dead, had been alive this whole time and was sitting by the fire. The pain of deception and disbelief hit her as she realized that meant her own father was the one who had sent Ian after her. He was the one who hadn't cared if she lived or died when he'd sold her to Ian.

"Hello, Father."

Jane enjoyed the look of surprise as her father's head shot up from the book he was reading. Jane sat in the old worn leather high back chair across from him and gave him a little wave.

"Jane? What are you doing here?" Her father looked to the open door and relaxed when he didn't see anyone else.

"I thought I'd visit. It's been what? Four hundred years? So, what are you up to?" Jane tried to control her anger as she stared at the man who had betrayed her for her whole life.

"How did you get here?"

"I used the front door. You should really think about locking it. You never know who could just walk right in," Jane said with a slight scold and loved the way her father's face turned red. "I actually came here to ask you a question."

"How did you know I was here?" Anwir Farrington asked.

Jane shrugged. "I know a lot of things. I know you partnered with Alexander to orchestrate the uprising and take control of the council. I know Aunt Loralei was Alexander's mistress. I know the stone keeper told you my match to Ian wasn't good but you ignored her. So, I came to ask you why. Why did you do it? Why did you commit treason and kill so many of your own kind? Why did you sell your daughter to a horrible man who only wanted to steal my powers? Why, Father?"

Her father looked toward the door again and relaxed once more when he didn't see anyone there. He probably thought she was dumb enough to come alone.

"I guess you inherited your mother's poor powers after all. You didn't even set off the protection spell for anyone using magic," her father sneered, finally letting the pure loathing he had for her show.

"You're right. I did inherit Mother's powers. Tell me why, Father. You owe me that much." Jane felt remarkably calm as she faced the man who had destroyed their family and so many other families so callously.

"Owe *you*? You owe me. You were supposed to be a son, but your pathetic mother couldn't even get that right. I married her when my previous relationship was fruitless and your mother swore she could give me an heir. Instead, all she gave me was a girl as worthless as she was. Why did I sell you to Ian?" Her father laughed as if it were funny. "That was the least you owed *me*! Then you had your little friend kill Ian and now my chance of taking over the council is slipping away. Well, it's not gone yet. I have one last play to make. Now, I think I'll take what's owed me—your powers. It's the only thing you're good for."

"Before you do, I thought I should tell you something," Jane said calmly. Even though her heart was beating hard she didn't show it.

"Jane?" her father jumped at the sound of Galen's voice.

"Don't worry, Father. It's just my husband. You can't take his powers. He's not a witch," Jane told her dad. "In here, Galen."

She smiled up at her husband as he walked into the room. "Hey. You must be Jane's father. I'm her husband. I didn't know Jane had any family left."

Her father looked disgusted as he didn't bother rising to meet Galen. "This is what you wanted to tell me? That you married a *human*," he said with disgust.

"No. I was going to tell you that the Farrington line dies with me." Jane gave him a little smile.

"The Farrington line will only grow and prosper. Things are in motion. Big things. It was a setback with the arrival of The One, but it's now time. Goodbye, Jane. Tell your mother I haven't thought of her once."

"I'm not human," Galen said suddenly as Anwir raised his hands. "I'm Keeper of the Stones of Stenness."

"I didn't expect that, but you'll die just the same as a human. Your grandmother was a meddlesome bitch. It'll be good to be rid of you all."

"You know what's interesting about being the Keeper?" Galen asked, ignoring Anwir's threat. "Reading the history of witches my Nan left behind. Did you know the council voted today to strip you of your name and your seat on the council? Jane wasn't lying when she said the Farrington line would end with her. Well, I guess she was lying a little bit."

"What does that mean?" Anwir shot to his feet and then suddenly he froze. There was a ripple in the protection. "You brought a witch with you. You stupid girl. Is your friend Zoey trying to save her father? It's too late. I've taken almost all of his power. I was saving the very last for the grand finale, but I guess I'll just kill him after he watches me drain the life from his daughter."

"Sit down, Father. I'm not done talking to you," Jane ordered.

Her father scoffed and turned to walk out the door. Jane let a fraction of her powers loose. They slammed into his back as she used them to pick him up and drop him back into his chair.

He gaped at her in disbelief before a greedy gleam showed in his eye. "Your power has grown. Ian's loss is my gain."

"My powers haven't grown, Father. They've been there all along. See, Mother gave me her powers and *her* mother's powers. I am The Kendrick now, with the full power of the original Kendrick family. Mother hid it from you. I hid it from you. Now you will tell me what this grand finale is or I'll take your power."

"I am The Farrington. The male line was always stronger than the Kendrick line."

"Actually, no. You're *a* Farrington."

"Don't try to claim to be a Farrington now, you traitor. I should have killed you as a babe!" her father yelled.

"But then I wouldn't have known Jane and she's become very important to me."

Jane smiled as Samuel walked into the room with Polly by his side.

"If you're keeping track, Father, I'm The Kendrick, Polly is The Lurie, and Samuel here, well, I'll let him explain." Jane stood and joined her brother.

With a nod of her head, she sent Galen searching for the rest of the council. It was time for her father to face those he had tried to destroy.

Her father scoffed at Samuel. "You're that Mannering brat. You have no power here."

"The Mannerings were my parents. Until you killed them," Samuel admitted.

"Darwin was right when he said only the strong would survive."

The room began to fill with people. Jane watched as her father got more and more agitated.

"Hello, Anwir. Can't say I'm happy to see you again," Vilma said, crossing her arms and glaring at him.

"Where's your bitch of a sister?" Anwir spat.

"Right here," Agnes said, looking very spry for someone as old as she. And very pissed. Agnes looked ready to blast Anwir from existence.

Then Jane saw why. Magnus Rode was in Slade's arms before he gently lowered the man to the ground, but Slade still had his arm around Magnus's back to keep him on his feet. Galen hurried forward and took over for Slade. Jane saw his hands light up as he ran them over the man who had been like a father to her since she moved to Moonshine Hollow.

Zoey was glowing, and if Agnes looked mad, Zoey looked ready to do major destruction.

"While Magnus was under your roof," Lauren said, stepping forward with Slade at her side. "Slade and I have been making some discoveries. I assume your daughter told you that you've been found guilty of the kidnap and rape of Khepri Katz?"

"I'm pleased to inform you we've stripped you of all rights to the council and now that we have you in person, we'll be taking your powers as well," Slade said with such menace Jane shivered.

"If you tell us what you have planned, we'll let you live," Jane said, knowing she'd overstepped the grand master and mistress, but she had to find out what this grand finale was.

"The plan is simple, daughter. Your time is up. The era of the Farrington rule is here. You'll never find me until I'm standing over your dead bodies." Her father went to transport but couldn't.

"Leaving so soon? I wouldn't hear of it, especially as I've learned this new trick," Zoey said with a cold smile. "Turns out I can block transport too."

"By rights of birth, do you wish to take the Farrington power?" Slade asked. Jane knew he was asking Samuel as the eldest Farrington, but her father didn't realize that.

"Even if Jane is The Kendrick, she doesn't have the power to strip me of my powers," Anwir scoffed. Jane could see his fingers twitching. He was ready for the fight.

"I wasn't talking to Jane," Slade said dismissively. "Samuel, the call is yours."

"Samuel? He's a Mannering! He isn't strong enough to stir a breeze," Anwir laughed.

"We were interrupted when we were discussing my parents," Samuel said coldly. "I was raised by the Mannering family, but they weren't my birth parents. See, my mother had been kidnapped and raped. The stone keeper kept her safe and helped deliver me into this world. Right before my mother died, she gave me all her powers. I am The Katz."

Jane watched as her father's mouth dropped open and then slammed shut. "My son. You're my son," he said before laughing. "I did it! Now we'll be unstoppable!"

"There's one problem," Samuel said, stopping their father's glee. "I was born in the light of the Goddess, not the darkness in which you operate. I don't want his powers, Master Slade. I want them destroyed. The Farrington line is at its end."

Jane almost felt sorry for her father as he looked around and realized there was no getting out of this. Jane saw his hands move and she acted without thinking. Her powers slammed into her father. She felt her mother's hand on hers as centuries of pain and suffering coursed through her to finally deliver justice.

Her father stumbled back and fired back. His powers were darkened by black magic, but when Samuel and the rest of the council joined in, Anwir Farrington realized he was going to lose everything. His powers were torn from his body as Zoey let loose her fifth element. The white light encircled the Farrington powers and then they simply vanished. The Farrington line was at an end.

"Stop!" Lauren ordered.

His powers were almost completely gone and in his place was the shell of an old human.

"You'll never hurt me or any witch again," Jane told him.

"Let him live in this sorry state. Bind him so he can't use what little he has left. Without his powers, he'll die alone. My mother and Khepri will have their justice."

Neferu glared down at him with loathing. "Khepri was like a daughter to me. I would have killed you."

"Let's go," Jane said, slipping her hand into Samuel's. "He's not worth another thought."

Jane and Samuel turned, leaving the old man who had ruined the lives of so many families sitting helpless in the chair.

"No!" Neferu screamed.

Wind shot through the room, knocking Jane into Samuel. They both stumbled back, and as Jane turned she saw her father, knife in hand, frozen in the air. He'd tried to stab her in the back. Wind swirled as Neferu's anger grew. Then with a sickening crack, the wind died as Anwir's broken body was dropped to the ground.

"I told you I'd kill you," Neferu said coldly. She'd used the wind to break his neck when he went after Jane. "You'll never hurt another Claritase again."

"Jane! Are you okay, love?" Galen was by her side in a heartbeat, worry on his face.

"I'm fine. Let's go home to Moonshine Hollow. I just want to be around our kind and see them happy and safe once again."

Jane gave one last look as Raiden and Niles picked up her father. They'd take care of things here. Fern was staying as well. They would go through the papers and books to bring anything relevant home for the history books.

The sound of children laughing caught Jane's attention as they walked out the front door. She turned and saw an image of Samuel chasing two little toddlers. "Samuel, this place is yours now."

"I don't want it," her brother said with a shake of his head.

"But it wants you. You'll change it, rename it, clear it out, and make it a happy place filled with children," Jane smiled as the image faded.

"A country house does sound kind of nice," Polly said with a smile as she placed her hand over her stomach. "I bet there's even a stable."

The Farrington curse was over. There would be happiness here again.

16

"My grandchild," Magnus said with wonder as he placed his hand on Zoey's abdomen. He was still recovering but was now able to walk on his own as his powers regenerated. He'd hidden the special power he'd been developing. But even as powerful as it was, it still would take a couple more days of Agnes feeding him her special smoothies until he was back to normal.

"Our grandchild," Zoey's mother said with a smile as she sat with her husband, Bradley. They were all celebrating the pregnancy news because the first thing her father did upon returning to Moonshine Hollow was to ask Samuel to go get Zoey's mother and stepfather so they could celebrate.

"It's going to be a very special child," Magnus said, not for the first time.

"Is that how you felt with me, Mom?" Zoey teased.

"Oh yes. I knew you were going to be special from the moment you were conceived. I think every parent has that feeling. That instantaneous love and pride you develop is something else," her mother said with a soft smile as if she remembered the feeling of carrying Zoey. "And how much fun is it that you all are pregnant together?"

Polly and Jane nodded. "Zoey gets to tell us all the fun things to expect," Polly told them.

"It's been so long since we've had witchlings, I think everyone is being great, but a little witchling-crazed." Jane looked pointedly at Lauren, who was working with Neferu on lesson plans for the school.

Zoey laughed, but then cocked her head. "What's that noise?"

The packed house went quiet. Zoey listened and heard it again. It was growing louder and louder as it blasted through the air.

"Tornado siren!" Agnes yelled. "Get into the basement!"

Slade had her hand in his as they rushed toward the basement door. "Let the air witches handle it," he called back at her when Zoey tugged on his hand to stop him. How he knew she wanted to help was beyond her, but that was exactly what she wanted to do.

Bradley was helping Magnus down the stairs when Zoey heard it.

Laughter.

Everyone except Bradley and her mother froze.

"This isn't a tornado," Zoey said, feeling the tendrils of black magic whipping through the air. Zoey opened her senses and let her power travel to check on the town like she did every morning. She heard the booming claps of thunder and the earth shaking from strikes of lightning as she felt the fear of witches and humans alike.

"Whoever is the force behind the dark magic is here," Zoey said with no emotion. It was time to fight. There wasn't time for emotion.

"I guess it wasn't my dad, then," Jane said as she, too, got ready to fight.

"Whoever it is, I'm tired of this. I am so tired of this." Zoey tugged her hand from Slade's and marched through the living room. "Bradley, take Mom and Dad to the basement to keep them safe. We have a naughty witch to deal with."

"Sweetness," Slade called out, but Zoey was already yanking open the front door.

"It's time, Slade. Can't you feel it?" Zoey had to yell over the howling winds.

"We make our stand now," Slade hollered as he reached for her.

Zoey tried to transport to downtown, but couldn't. Transport was blocked, just like it had been at Farrington Castle and just like it had been at the uprising. "We walk together. Let's end this."

The wind pushed them in every direction as they forced their way down the street. "Get inside!" Zoey screamed at neighbors and friends who were coming outside to see the unnatural storm. Finally they reached Main Street where humans and witches alike huddled inside the brick buildings on Main Street.

When other witches saw the council they came out to join them. Zoey saw fear in their eyes as the tornado formed at the other end of Main Street. It ripped the steeple from the church as it bore down on them.

Wind, debris, and maniacal laughter filled the town. Windows were blown out or benches thrown through them. People screamed as they held on for their lives.

"Air witches get ready!" Neferu ordered as if she'd spent

centuries on the battlefield, which she had. Witches planted their feet wide and called up their powers.

Black lightning mixed with light blue air power as the battle for Moonshine Hollow, the Claritase, and the Tenebris began.

"Show yourself!" Zoey yelled into the sky. She slowly circled around, looking for the person behind the dark magic. "You're nothing but a coward, hiding behind evil. If you think you're so powerful, show yourself!"

A black lightning bolt shot from the sky, but Zoey was ready. She shot it with her white power and turned to continue her taunts. "You're nothing without Ian! Was he the power behind this and now you're mad because I killed him?"

A scream answered her, but it wasn't the scream she expected. This one came from Clara as she was ripped from the doorway at her boutique. She was flung through the air like a ragdoll.

"I got her!" Neferu yelled as she fought back the wind to get Clara back onto her feet.

"Oh, thank you," Clara cried as she clutched at Neferu's tunic.

"Neferu!" Zoey screamed as the black tendrils reached out from Clara's hand and shot into Neferu's heart.

Neferu's head dropped back as a scream tore through her throat and out her mouth. Clara laughed the same menacing laugh that had been torturing them.

"No!" Zoey yelled, the white light shooting from her fingers and slamming into Clara.

Niles roared a battle cry that harkened back to old Scotland as Lauren joined Zoey in attacking Clara.

Niles charged forward, lowered his shoulder, and took

both women down to the ground. The hit knocked Clara's hold on Neferu loose enough for Niles to grab her.

"Isn't she a little old for you?" Clara chuckled. "However, I love a strong young man. Don't I, Aggie?"

Agnes sucked in a breath at the nickname. "Only one person ever called me that."

"As little witchlings, we talked of growing old. But oh my, did you and Vilma turn really old. I've managed to keep my youthful looks. Good genes I guess," Clara said as if they were two old friends simply chatting. Clara ignored the group of witches surrounding her as she turned to take in the people in the crowd. "There's little Janie. Now you're all grown up and married to the stone keeper. I bet your father had a fit when he learned of that before you killed him."

"I killed him," Neferu said as she leaned on Niles to stand. "And I'll kill you too."

"You were always such a cold witch," Clara said with a roll of her eyes.

"Who are you?" Jane asked as The Six moved to stand next to each other.

"You don't recognize me? I'm hurt. Maybe this will help." Clara reached for her ear and slowly began to peel away her face. Her blonde hair was pulled back along with the face as she stripped the human suit from her body. In her place stood a woman who looked to be in her thirties, with shining jet-black hair and eyes just as dark.

"Aunt Loralei?" Jane gasped.

"An added benefit of tapping into the dark arts, I can stay young forever. I can also change form. I've been living here, listening, observing, and you all were too weak to even know it. I was always underestimated. Not anymore. Bow to me," Loralei Farrington yelled. "Swear your allegiance to me and I'll let you live. Deny me and you can die as I make the humans my slaves."

Zoey didn't give anyone time to think about Loralei's demand. Instead, she blasted her with her power. Loralei turned and shot back. Their energies fought for control as Loralei laughed.

Zoey felt the power in Loralei. She felt the darkness, the evil, and the price she'd paid with her soul to become so powerful. As one, The Six turned their powers on Loralei. Even as Zoey knew Jane must have been dying inside from the betrayal, she fought by Zoey's side.

Loralei made an X with her arms. Zoey saw the dark magic gathering and then Loralei shot her arms up into the air. Zoey and all the witches were thrown backward from the dark energy bomb.

A wall was erected with a flick of Loralei's hand. The Six were cut off from the rest of the town. Behind the wall sat Main Street. Behind The Six were the neighborhoods to one side and Earnest Park to the other.

"Aunt Loralei," Jane called out as she scrambled up to her feet. "Why are you doing this?"

Loralei rolled her dark eyes as Zoey and the others got to their feet.

"We have to lead her away from the citizens," Slade whispered into Zoey's ear.

Zoey nodded and reached for Polly's hand. She gave a slight tug and they all took a step toward the park as Loralei stalked forward.

"Why? Men and women have always been equal because you could never have one without the other. Claritase and Tenebris were equal in their powers. But then humans messed it all up. Why? *Power*, my little Janie. Human males wanted it and so they took it. They turned human women into nothing more than property, bought and sold for land or money. They had no life outside of their houses," Loralei ranted as she shot black energy at their feet, laughing as The Six jumped backward.

"I was sick of it. I was a powerful witch in my own right and suddenly Tenebris True Loves were thinking we Claritase needed to bow down to them. I don't think so. I never bow to anyone— man, woman, or Goddess. So I changed the world."

"How? All you did was kill thousands of innocents," Jane yelled as they continued to walk backward into the park.

Loralei shrugged, "Sometimes a few bystanders have to die in a revolution. I found Alexander, who believed as I do: witches are the apex species. I made the conversation not man versus woman, but witch versus human. We were done letting humans set the tone for society and history. It was our time to make Earth a witch society with humans as our servants."

"Alexander was with my mother though, wasn't he? Or did your affair start before then?" Slade asked as the ground transitioned from pavement to grass under Zoey's feet.

"You council members. You always think you know everything when you all fail to look at the big picture. Who do you think introduced Helena to Alexander? I did. Who do you think caused their separation after she was with child? I did. Who do you think whispered to Anwir to get that Katz bitch pregnant? I did. Too bad it didn't work out and he had to do with Aurora Kendrick. But I did that too. A little whisper here, a little whisper there. A nudge, a comment, a diary accidently left out . . . they were all so stupid. Everything Alexander and Anwir did was because of me. A woman."

"You would control the next generation who had the

power of the six original council members and take over the council in order to elevate yourself into power?" Zoey asked as they slowly walked backward into the field. She could hear the running water behind her as thunder and lightning still crackled over the town behind Loralei.

"Of course it's about power. I'm tired of hiding. I'm tired of pretending witches don't exist and that humans are superior. They're so far beneath us they should thank us for even allowing them to breathe our same air. As soon as Alexander had Slade in his control, he and I were to be together. We were going to be the rulers of a new race of witches. No more Claritase and Tenebris. Alexandertons. The legacy of the combining of Alexander and the Farrington line was to be the new name of the witches who joined us. No more male, no more female. Just one group led by Alexander and me."

"What happened?" Jane asked. "You took me to Ian the night of the fighting and I never saw you again."

"I took you to Ian so he could use your powers to defeat the Claritase and the Tenebris who refused to support Alexander. When I got back, I found your father wounded. He wasn't dead though. Alexander was winning, but then I was hit. It interrupted my concentration on the transport blocking spell. In a blink, everyone was gone. I spend the next four hundred years ferreting out names and locations of Claritase survivors and giving them to Hunters. I even found the last Rode, but Slade couldn't even do a simple job properly. After Slade disappeared like the miserable coward he is, I took my place by Alexander's side. Until Zoey came along."

Zoey had hoped she'd continue to talk, but Loralei had some anger to work out. The black bolt of energy shot into

Zoey, knocking her across the field. Her back slammed into the post of the bridge and she groaned in pain.

"After Alexander died I knew that my time had finally come. I'd begun an affair with Ian and actually fell in love with him. He was my True Love. Then my own niece killed him." Loralei shot Jane with another bolt of black energy.

Zoey watched as her friend flew through the air and slammed into the post opposite Zoey. Jane fought to catch the air that was knocked out of her lungs.

"I'm done waiting. The time has come for the next generation of rule. *My rule.* You'll all die, the end of the original six families, well, except Samuel. I don't know why you're here, Mannering, but you'll die anyway. The rest of the witches will beg to be one of my subjects once the power of the council is gone."

Slade and Galen had backpedaled quickly so they could get to Zoey and Jane. Polly and Samuel took position between them and Loralei.

"Let's wash this town free of you and I can begin my reign." Loralei flicked her wrist as the wind picked back up and the water began to rise as The Six struggled to stand at the entrance to the bridge. Loralei turned toward the town and send black magic flying into the sky. Clouds gathered and crashed together. Black lightning shot behind the wall and then Zoey saw it. The flicker of flames. She heard the screams as Moonshine Hollow was set on fire. Loralei laughed and Zoey knew their time was up.

17

"The vision! This is the last stand," Zoey said, reaching up to grip Slade's hand.

Zoey reached for Jane and soon The Six were standing at the entrance of the bridge with their hands linked.

"Aren't you cute," Loralei laughed as she aimed her hands at them and fired a taunting shot of energy. It knocked into the mountain behind them, sending boulders crashing down. There would be no escape across the bridge.

"Together," Zoey called out. "Now!"

The Six fought back as one. White, green, red, and blue energy crashed into the darkness as the battle began in earnest. Galen stood next to Jane with his hand on her shoulder. He was offering support and whatever power the stone keeper could during a fight.

Loralei laughed, but the laughter stopped when Samuel dropped to the ground and shot out Loralei's feet. Loralei stumbled back and cursed. "You have more power than a Mannering, Samuel. Who are you?"

"I'm Samuel Mannering Katz, son of Khepri Katz. My mother sends her regards."

"That's not possible!" Loralei shouted as Samuel's battle cry roared out as the fullness of the Katz power was released. He felt generations of dormant power bursting free as if it had been caged far too long and now desperate for escape.

Slade stepped forward and joined Samuel as they pushed Loralei back. She stumbled and fell and Zoey was ready to take her down. "Come on powers," she muttered, trying to call up the next level powers she'd unlocked the other day, only they weren't coming.

Loralei caught herself and laughed. "You're strong, but I know your weakness. It's your friendship and your love."

Loralei turned and shot Jane with a bolt of black energy right in her stomach. "Your children. Watch as I destroy your True Loves and your little brats."

Zoey's hand moved automatically to protect her baby, as did Polly's. Galen stepped in front of Jane and took the second hit of black energy meant to kill their child.

The men roared. The women grew cold and quiet. Zoey saw Polly glowing red and Jane glowing green. When she looked down, Zoey saw her white glowing brighter than she'd ever seen it before.

A power stronger than True Love. Zoey had her answer. It was the love for your child.

Zoey reached for Jane who reached for Polly. With her other hand she reached for Slade. The Six came together as one. It hurt to hold back the energy surging forward, but she had to wait for the right time. Jane's hand was squeezing Zoey's so hard she was sure bones would be broken, but they *knew*. They knew they had one shot to defeat Loralei and they couldn't waste it.

Loralei laughed again. "I've been growing my powers for

a millennium and you think you can stop me? Let me show you what I can do."

The blast of dark power encircled them. It squeezed in from all directions. Zoey felt it crawling along her skin reaching for her baby and for her heart. "Now!"

Zoey released her powers. White light burst forward like an explosion. Her body shook, her muscles cramped, and she was sure she was screaming as their powers shot out to battle the evil surrounding them. Light and dark. Good and evil. The battle raged all around them.

Zoey didn't want to doubt herself or her friends, but Loralei was strong. The thunder clapped over them and, as their powers lit up the sky, the water began to rise. Zoey felt it covering her feet and when the blood rain began she knew what was next.

It was taking all her strength to battle the darkness. There was no way she could stop the blood tsunami she knew was coming.

The earth rumbled with the power of the wave racing toward them.

Polly dropped to her knees. The struggle to fight wore on. As they battled, Galen used the stone keeper's power to try to keep the darkness away from them. Jane's whole body shook next to Zoey's. Zoey couldn't tell if the blood on Jane's face was from overusing her powers or the blood rain pounding down upon them. The dark, thick clouds obscured any light. The only way they could see was with their own powers lighting up the sky around them before smashing into the darkness of Loralei's energy.

"I will level this town and everyone in it. Maybe I'll take Slade as my hostage," Loralei laughed. "I've had his father and cousin. The beefcake would be a nice addition to my trophy case."

Zoey's body began to shake. It shook with anger and it shook with exhaustion. She didn't know how much longer she could keep it up, but she had to. She had to protect her baby, she had to protect her True Love, and she had to protect her friends.

Zoey saw the bolt of dark energy shoot toward her. "No!" Zoey yelled. She tried to jump out of the way, but the bolt never hit her. Slade fell as he took the hit protecting her.

"Now who will protect you and your baby?" Loralei laughed.

"I will," a cold voice roared a moment before a baseball bat slammed into Loralei's head from behind her. "No one hurts *my* baby or grandbaby!"

"*Mom!*" Zoey gasped in shock as Loralei fell to the ground. There her mother stood, a petite warrior in a tailored dark pink suit with pearls at her neck and ears, ready to commit murder with a baseball bat to protect her child and grandchild.

In that one moment Loralei's powers dropped. It was all the time they needed. Zoey advanced on her. She ran, hands outstretched, as her powers encircled Loralei. Behind her, Slade rose and together The Six raced forward. With the last of their power they formed a circle around Loralei as witches began appearing all around them. Citizens of Moonshine Hollow were running, carrying guns, frying pans, and hunting knives as they prepared to leap into the battle to save Moonshine Hollow.

Zoey turned to her left and clasped Slade's hand. She turned to her right and clasped Galen's hand. Together they tightened the circle, directing their powers at Loralei. She had gotten to her knees and was fighting back with all she had, but the tide had turned.

"Feel the love, Jellybean. Feel your powers growing from

it," her father said from behind her as she felt his hand rest on her shoulder. The deep strum of his powers, a gift of love from the Goddess, flowed through her. She felt her mother's hand rest on her other shoulder as Jane's Aunt Eileen joined her. Friends, loved ones, council members, witches, and humans—all reached forward to give a supporting hand to The Six.

Galen began to chat in the old language. Only this time it appeared everyone understood it. The chant of love, healing, and friendship filled the valley up to the top of the mountains. Loralei screamed as if her soul was being torn from her body. A human-shaped dark, oily figure began to separate from Loralei's form.

Galen chanted louder as The Six used their powers to keep the figure contained within the circle. A horrendous sound of the dark magic being fully separated from Loralei's soul turned Zoey's stomach. The darkness didn't give in as Loralei collapsed. Instead it fought. It fought for a new host, but then Galen's hands began to glow. His light was like a shock to the dark magic. It screeched an unnatural sound as Galen fought it back.

"Now, Zoey," her father yelled over the screaming.

Zoey pulled from deep inside her. The last of her powers shot forward. Her body was near exhaustion. She didn't know if it was the blood rain or the exertion of using all her powers that was causing blood to run down her face from her nose, ears, and probably even her eyes. The amount of power it took to try to defeat Loralei felt as if it would kill Zoey. The white energy formed a circle with nothing but darkness in the center of it as it whirled forward. Galen was trembling. His body was wracked with tremors as Lauren and Niles held him up from behind. They had the evil pinned, but they wouldn't last much longer.

"There must be balance between good and evil, light and dark. With the night comes the dawn," Zoey said although the words weren't coming from her. She was the conduit for them from something much more powerful. "The Fifth Element is that balance. She is lightness and darkness working in harmony. Your time of evil is over."

It felt as if Zoey was struck by lightning. Energy surged through her from every direction. The circle of light with the swirling black center grew brighter and darker at the same time. It grew and grew until it was almost blinding. The dark figure shrieked, and then with one last push of Zoey's hands, her fifth element engulfed the figure.

"*Zoey!*" She heard Slade, her mother, and father scream before she collapsed unconscious on the blood covered ground.

∿

"Zoey, honey, can you hear me?"

"Bradley?" Zoey asked, blinking her eyes open. The sun was out and perfect white fluffy clouds were floating across the bright blue sky above her.

Faces swarmed her vision. Her stepfather had a blood pressure cuff on her and was looking down at her calmly as Galen used his hands to scan her for injuries.

Bradley used a penlight to test her eyes. "Can you tell how many fingers I'm holding up?" Bradley asked in full doctor mode. She saw her father holding on to her mother as they looked worriedly down at her with everyone else.

It was then she realized her head was in Slade's lap. "Welcome back, sweetness. Can you tell Bradley how many fingers he'd holding up?"

"One," she answered.

"Good," Bradley said before running her through a complete neurological exam. "I don't think you have a concussion. I think you used up all your powers and passed out from exhaustion."

"Is it gone? Where's Loralei?" Zoey asked, struggling to sit up.

"It's over," Slade told her. "You took care of it with a little help from the Goddess."

"Loralei didn't make it. Evil had fed on her until nothing was left. When it left her body, Loralei died," Jane said as she took a seat on the grass next to her.

Zoey reached out to clasp her friend's hand when Agnes appeared with one of her magical smoothies and shoved it into her mouth.

"*Howd hm bown?*" Zoey tried to say but was muffled by the drink Agnes was forcing on her.

"She asked how's the town," Bradley told everyone. "I'm used to patients trying to speak with they have things in their mouth."

"It's saved, thanks to y'all," Maribelle called out. "As soon as your mama hit that witch with the baseball bat, her powers holding us captive evaporated. The witches were gone in a blink, but we had to make a run to get here. We weren't going to let that evil witch take you or this town from us."

Agnes finally pulled the drink from her mouth and Zoey was able to reach for her mother. "You are a warrior woman in pearls," Zoey said, taking hold of her mother's hand.

"I would do anything to protect my child. Even take on an evil being. And *never* underestimate a woman in pearls," her mother said through a teary smile

"So, that was the Goddess? I knew what I was saying, but it wasn't me saying it. Then the power I felt. Wow. It was intense." Zoey struggled to sit up. Slade helped her up and she leaned against his chest as she took a deep breath.

"It was. Nothing like that has happened since the first Grand Mistress. I believe you're the Goddess's chosen one. You should be grand mistress," Lauren said, bowing her head to Zoey.

"That's not what I felt," Zoey said with a little smile. There was something she had heard, but hadn't said out loud. It wasn't for anyone but her. *You're the balance of good and evil. You are the Keeper of the Balance. Your daughter will fill your role after you and then your granddaughter after her. You will start a long history of powerful Rode women. And your sons, well, they will be blessed with the kindness and goodness of their grandmother and the strength, determination, and fairness of their father. The Habsburg line will become leaders of the world. Your service, the service of your family, the service of The Six, and the families of The Six, in the name of good, will bring in a new generation of witches—a generation of one.*

"What did you feel?" Lauren asked.

"I'm not to be the grand mistress. I'm to be the Keeper of the Balance. My daughters and I will be responsible for keeping the balance between good and evil and between light and dark in the world. Also, I think the Goddess gave me permission to change things going forward. We're going to have a very interesting council meeting," Zoey said with a laugh.

18

It had taken a week for Zoey and Magnus to fully recover, but recover they did. Now Zoey was glowing with the enhanced powers the Goddess left behind along with her pregnancy glow. Her stomach had just begun to round, and while the council had worked nonstop, Zoey had never felt better.

The town of Moonshine Hollow was preparing for the largest Halloween party they'd ever thrown. After finding out it was evil masquerading as Clara, who was fueling the anti-witch movement, the few hesitant residents joined the rest of the town in welcoming the Claritase and Tenebris. Today they'd instructed all the witches to stay out of town until six at night, which worked perfectly since it was time for the largest joint meeting of witches in five hundred years.

"Nervous?" Slade asked as he slipped his arm around her.

"Very. Do you think they'll be receptive to our ideas?" Zoey looked out at the crowd gathered in Earnest Park. Every witch on the globe was there. Niles and Neferu had recorded the newest history within the official records. As such, each witch's history book pinged with a new entry, almost like email. They learned about the traitors, they learned about The Six, they learned about the Goddess assigning the role of Keeper of the Balance to Zoey, and they learned Moonshine Hollow was a safe place for them. They were invited by Lauren and Magnus to attend a meeting this afternoon to settle on the future of their kind.

As Lauren scanned the crowd, she noted it was smaller than it had been five hundred years ago, but it was full of life. Witches were hugging witches. People were crying tears of joy after hiding their powers for centuries.

"We'll find out," Slade said as Lauren stepped up to the podium in Earnest Park.

"Claritase and Tenebris, welcome to Moonshine Hollow!" Lauren called out with the largest, happiest smile Zoey had ever seen on her face. Beside her, Zoey's father was similarly smiling and clapping. "You've all read the history account from the last month. What you haven't read is the two councils have been working nonstop with the message the Goddess imparted to Mistress Zoey. We've reached a decision that will change our kind forever."

Lauren paused as the witches began to whisper. She held up her hands to calm them.

"You've got this," Slade whispered in her ear before giving her a kiss as Lauren called her to the stage.

The thunderous applause surprised Zoey as she made the way to the podium. The councils moved to stand in a line behind her.

"The Goddess told me we'd start a new generation of witches. A generation of one. I believe, with all my heart, that it means the end of the Claritase and Tenebris," Zoey said and wasn't surprised when noise erupted. She gave them time and didn't continue until they quieted down to turned their attention back to her. "Loralei Farrington talked about uniting everyone under Alexander. She meant to use you as servants to their power. However, we only defeated those traitors by working together. We are stronger together. Together we hold each other accountable. Together we learn more, we push each other to be better, and we do good. Together we can change the world. So that's what I proposed to the council. We merge the Claritase and Tenebris into one. We move forward, together."

There were gasps, excited chatter, and even clapping.

"The councils have voted and we now ask for your vote. We move to form a new group, a single group of witches called Claribris. Two halves of our names made into one, just like us," Zoey said. She scanned the crowd for reactions and was pleased to see no angry faces, just excited witches, all listening intently.

"Moonshine Hollow will house the Council of The Six and the Grand Master or Grand Mistress," Zoey said, continuing. "The Council of The Six will consist of the Stone Keeper of Stenness and the five original council member lines. Our job will be to help you all with your calling. Leadership, education, healing, art, science, or whatever it is you wish to contribute to make the world a better place. You are no longer relegated to the outskirts of society. We want you to become public faces. They just don't need to know about the magical aspect of us," Zoey said as the audience gave a little laugh.

"You can run for president, you can audition for Broadway, you can write a book, you can follow your passion. The rules will be as follows. There is to be no use of magic to further your passion. When using magic to help others, do so in a way they don't know it. That rule hasn't changed. The use of magic will be to the benefit of society only, not to yourselves.

"The stone keeper will advise on your magical health and the health of humans. I will advise on the balance of good and evil, such as how to handle the trickier cases of punishment versus protection. I'll work closely with Master Samuel who will advise on protection and uses for air magic. Master Slade will advise on leadership and water magic. Mistress Jane will advise on adventure and earth magic. Mistress Polly will advise on kindness and fire magic. Further, instead of two leaders, only one will be chosen. You will elect that leader along with a panel of thirteen elected officials who fill the role of the Claribris Council. They will record the history, hear petitions, make rules, and hand out punishments."

Zoey took a deep breath and gave the audience a nod. They cheered as she stepped back from the podium and her father took her place. "Good job, Jellybean," he whispered as he hugged her.

"I am Magnus Rode, the head of the Tenebris until your vote. We will be taking an hour-long recess and then we will vote on the motion. If that passes, the new council will get a new leader. There are some changes you should be aware of before you make your nominations. I hereby resign my position as leader of the Tenebris and refuse any nomination to the leadership. I am taking a new job. I'll be the principal of the Moonshine Hollow Witchling School. If you're interested in teaching little witchlings, please see me after the meeting."

Zoey watched her father step down from the podium as the witches stood from their seats and conversation erupted.

Today was the first day of their new history and it filled Zoey will pride and excitement to watch.

The council members were mobbed by witches with questions and with introductions to witches from around the world. The next generation was excited to move forward into a new age.

Magnus returned to the podium after an exciting hour. Zoey held Slade's hand as she waited for the future to be laid out. "We start with the vote of combining into one group."

With a wave of his hand a large jumbotron screen appeared behind the stage. "Please cast your vote."

Zoey watched as the vote went in favor of combining into one group, by an overwhelming margin. With a rap of his gavel, her father brought about a new age—the age of the Claribris.

"We move on with the nomination for our leader. Raise your hand and state your nomination," Magnus called out after a round of cheers went up for the new Claribris.

The nominations began. Lauren was nominated along with several other witches from across the globe. "Witches make your mark on the screen and cast your vote," Magnus told them.

Zoey looked at the board and with a flick of her finger placed her vote for Lauren.

"The first leader of the new Claribris is Grand Mistress Lauren!" Magnus said as cheers erupted.

Tears glistened in Lauren's eyes as she stepped forward. "I hereby accept with the condition that we vote every decade. My time as grand mistress is near its end, but I have a feeling there will be a new generation ready to take my place." Lauren looked to Zoey, Jane, and Polly. Zoey placed her hand over her baby bump and smiled.

"My first act as your grand mistress it to establish our council," Lauren said, turning back into the leader she'd been for the past centuries. Soon a group of thirteen members were chosen. Agnes and Vilma had turned down their nominations. Instead, they decided they wanted to devote their time to teach little witchlings. Fern, Raiden, Niles, and Neferu were voted on, along with new members from all over the world.

"The first meeting of the Claribris is now complete. The town of Moonshine Hollow has invited us all to a Halloween celebration, if you'd like to attend," Lauren told them to the cheers of the crowd.

"They do know we aren't so fond of Halloween, right?" Neferu said, crossing her arms over her chest and glaring down Main Street. It was decorated with so many Halloween decorations it bordered on grotesque, but Zoey loved every one of them.

A little girl came skipping up to them. She was in a witch's hat and a long black wig. She looked like a cross between a cute witch and a member of the Addams Family. She was completely adorable.

"Miss Neferu, can you guess what I am for Halloween?" she asked as she wiggled her fingers.

"A witch?" Neferu said with no enthusiasm.

"Well, I guess I am. But I'm you!"

Neferu's eyebrows shot up as she took a closer look at the witch costume. "Is that the Egyptian symbol for air?"

The little girl nodded. "Uh-huh. My momma said you were raised during that time. I love all things Egyptian. You're my favorite witch."

Neferu bent down to her level and with a little wiggle of her fingers made a tiny tornado, no more than three inches high, that jumped into the little girl's open hand. She giggled as she watched it dance there for a moment and then threw her arms around Neferu. "Thank you! That's the best gift ever."

Then she turned and skipped away.

Neferu stood and cleared her throat. "Well, maybe Halloween isn't so bad."

Zoey laughed as Main Street turned into a block party of witches doing tricks for the children, of the children giving witches their drawings, and of humans and witches learning from each other.

It was the perfect celebration to begin the new generation of the Claribris.

EPILOGUE

"Zoey! Let us in," Grand Mistress Lauren yelled through the magical barrier.

Zoey didn't respond. Instead, she clasped tightly to Slade's hand.

"That's it, lass. Just one more big push," Galen said calmly.

"This is the first witchling in over four hundred years! We need to document their arrival into the world," Lauren cried out before Slade wiggled his fingers and all outside noise was blocked.

Zoey had enough to think about as she delivered her baby. The remaining three from their group, the entire council, her parents, and half of Moonshine Hollow were waiting just outside the door for this baby to be born.

"You're doing great, sweetness," Slade whispered as he brushed back her sweat-soaked hair. She had thought labor would be easy for a witch. That she could just wiggle her fingers or say a spell and the baby would pop out. That, unfortunately, was not how it worked.

"Here we go," Galen said excitedly from between her propped up legs. "Push, Zoey. Now."

Zoey bore down, her body shining white from exertion. Lavender light filled the room as Zoey collapsed back against Slade's arms.

"It's a girl!" Galen said as he held up the little lavender bundle of light.

The baby inside the cocoon of light was looking around, her lavender eyes remarkably alert. Galen immediately put her on Zoey's chest as tears streamed down her cheeks.

Slade reached out and ran his finger over her chubby cheek. "Hello, sweetling. I'm your dad. Your mom and I have been waiting to meet you."

Zoey held out her finger and her daughter grabbed on to it. She was strong and, as she looked at Zoey, Zoey knew her father was right—this little girl was special.

Zoey watched as Slade and Galen cleaned the little girl up. Warmth filled her as Slade brought the baby over to her. "I feel the Goddess with us," Zoey whispered to Slade as he carried the sleeping bundle over to her.

"I feel my mother here, too," Slade said before he bent down and placed a soft kiss on the baby's forehead.

"I think I know what we should name her." Zoey told Slade her name as Galen helped her get ready for visitors.

"I love it," Slade said with a smile.

"I know I don't count, but I love it, too," Galen said with a smile. "Can I let them in?"

Zoey nodded as Slade handed the baby over to her and sat next to her on the bed. Her mother and father were the first through the door with Bradley, Lauren, Agnes, and Vilma very close behind.

"Tell us, everything!" Lauren said with happy tears running down her cheeks.

"I've got pictures," Galen said kindly. "I'll send them to you."

Zoey looked to Slade and gave him a nod. "It's a girl," Slade said with the largest smile she'd ever seen on his face before. Love, pride, and happiness radiated from his heart and soul.

"A girl," Zoey's mother said with a sigh. "Hand me my grandbaby right now. I can't stand another moment without her in my arms."

Zoey smiled as the baby opened her eyes. She focused on her grandmother's face and raised her hand. Zoey's mother became a blubbering mess of baby talk and noises as the lavender-eyed baby was placed in her arms.

"Do you have a name for the history book?" Neferu asked after being caught making funny faces at the baby.

This time it was Zoey who answered. "Helena Neve Rode."

Lauren dabbed at her eyes and let Helena clasp her finger. "Named after Slade's mother and Neve, meaning bright. The name has roots in an ancient Irish word for goddess. It's perfect. You're perfect, yes you are," Lauren cooed to Helena. "And this is just the beginning. Soon Moonshine Hollow will be filled with little witchlings."

The next hour flew by as all her friends, human and witch, came to visit. Love filled the room. Jane and Polly laughed and rubbed their very pregnant bellies. Several other witches were beginning to show in their new pregnancies as True Love matches were being made weekly at the new Moonshine Hollow Singles' Mingle. It had actually been Maribelle's idea. Witches from all over the world came together to dance, meet other witches, and in many cases, find their True Loves. Those True Loves had turned out to be mostly witches, but there were several witch and human True Loves now going strong.

Zoey looked to her own True Love and smiled. She looked down at their baby and kissed her forehead. Yes, things in Moonshine Hollow were very good and the best was yet to come.

~

Lauren looked around the full class of witchlings and her heart was full. After re-election to a second term, her time as Grand Mistress was growing to a close. This is where she belonged—in the school teaching witchlings how to use their powers for good.

"Can you believe that in the past sixteen years we have grown to have a full school house and are building others all over the world?" Magnus said, coming to stand by her on the first day of school.

"Hey, GML," Helena called out as she waved to Lauren and bounded up to give her grandfather a hug. The first witchling born in Moonshine Hollow had grown into a beautiful young witch. She had hair as dark as her father's, lavender eyes, and her mother's smile.

"Catherine Lurie, Ellis Katz," Lauren called out to the almost-sixteen-year-old twins of Samuel and Polly named after the Mannerings, who'd been Samuel's true parents. They bent down and told their three younger siblings to head inside the school before joining them.

"Morning, GML, Master M," they said, using the nicknames all the witchlings used for Grand Mistress Lauren and Master Magnus.

"Helena, you're looking hot today," Ellis said with a wink.

A football slammed into the back of Ellis's head. "Stop hitting on my sister, Ellis!" Helena's younger brother by a year, Graydon Habsburg yelled.

Helena wiggled her fingers and Ellis jumped. "You zapped me in the balls!"

Lauren hid her laugh under a scowl. "Helena, you don't zap men in the balls. Ellis, don't hit on her."

"Hi, Graydon," the quiet and sweet Tara Kendrick said as she joined them. "Happy first day of school."

"Oh, hi, Tara," Graydon said, suddenly shy. Lauren smiled, knowing True Love was in the air. They had time to realize it though. In the meantime, it was cute to watch Zoey and Slade's son be completely oblivious to the fact that Jane and Galen's daughter liked him.

"You think we have enough people to beat Moonshine Hollow High this year in basketball?" Mason Sinclair, Tara's older brother and the next Keeper of the Stones of Stenness asked Graydon and Ellis.

Lauren listened to the talking going on around her and felt at peace. Tonight she was stepping down as Grand Mistress at the yearly meeting. There would be a vote, but Slade Habsburg would become the next leader of the Claribris. It was fated.

Sixteen years was such a short time in a witch's life, but so much had changed. Witches were now a part of society. They were spreading goodness in the world at a time when it was needed the most. Sometimes it was just a smile to a stranger or letting a stranger go in front of them at the grocery store. Small acts of kindness had a big impact in people's lives when they needed it the most. Then there were the scientific breakthroughs, the CEOs, and the professionals doing kind deeds at work and for the world.

Every little ripple of kindness could be felt growing across the globe.

It hadn't been all happy endings. Zoey'd had to work to keep the balance several times, but now things were flowing well. Their powers sang with happiness and abundance. It was time for Lauren to move onto her next role as a teacher.

"Excuse me? Do you know where I can find Grand Mistress Lauren?"

Lauren turned from watching all the children walking into school to find a man standing there with a smile on his face. She felt it like a punch to her heart. She'd had her own True Love before. She couldn't possibly be feeling what she was feeling for this man. It had to be something else, yet she knew the feeling well even if her mind couldn't register it.

The man was tall. He looked to be about her human age, but who knew how old he was in witch years. His dark hair had just a hint of gray at the temples. His shoulders were wide, his waist narrow, and his thighs muscled. His eyes were silver, so not a witch. That didn't matter to her heart though. There were many happy witch-human True Loves. Her heart continued to beat wildly as she looked up at him.

"I'm Lauren. And you are?" she asked, proud her voice came out sounding normal and not like one of her love sick teenage witchlings.

"I'm Kamien, the Keeper of the Odry Stones from Poland. I'm the new teacher of the stones at the Claribris Witchling School."

Kamien held out his hand and when Lauren shook it, silver and teal sparks flew. "Oh my Goddess," Lauren muttered with disbelief as Kamien's silver eyes met hers in surprise.

. . .

"The Grand Mistress is kissing someone!" Catherine Lurie screamed out to her class.

"No way," Helena Rode said, jumping from her chair to join Catherine at the window.

"Wow, now *that's* a kiss. You sure you don't want to do that with me?" Ellis asked Helena, who zapped him in the balls again.

Graydon groaned. "Ellis, stop hitting on my sister! Whoa, that is one serious kiss."

"What is the meaning of this?" Neferu snapped as she walked into her classroom with Magnus by her side. "This is Air Power 301, not spying out the window."

"I think Grand Mistress Lauren found her True Love," Catherine called out.

Neferu paused for a second and then flew to the window, pushing witchlings out of the way. She smiled as she saw her friend glowing in the arms of a very handsome man. The kids were right. That was one serious kiss.

"That's enough. You wouldn't want someone spying on you when you find your True Love," Neferu said, walking back to join Magnus by the door. "Everyone, take out your text books and read the first chapter. I'll quiz you on it in ten minutes."

Neferu stepped out into the hall as Magnus closed the door. Agnes and Vilma came out of Beginner's Water Power and Earth Power 201.

"Did you all see it?" Agnes asked with a smile.

Neferu nodded and couldn't help the smile on her face.

"I knew when we met him at the last mingle he was perfect for Lauren," Vilma said with satisfaction.

"Magnus is the genius for hiring him to teach here," Neferu said with a nod of respect for Magnus.

"What can I say, I'm a True Love genius." Magnus gave a shrug and then they laughed. "How many is that now?"

Neferu opened the small book she carried. "Fern and Raiden were our first True Love matches we made. Then Niles and his True Love. We even found some True Love human and witch matches over the years. So, let's see. We've been doing this for sixteen years and we've matched"— Neferu scanned the pages and counted in her head — "one hundred and ninety-nine couples."

"We should do something special for two hundred," Agnes said.

"I agree. I already have two hundred lined up," Vilma told the secret matchmaking group. Vilma and Agnes shared a look as they glanced at Magnus and Neferu. The two were smiling at each other in that certain way. All they needed was a little push.

"Umph," Neferu grunted as she flew into Magnus's arms.

"Vilma, did you push me?" Neferu asked as Magnus held her in his arms.

"Me?" Vilma asked with wide innocent eyes. "Why would I push you?"

"Magnus, thank you for being a gentleman and catching me. My, but you are strong," Neferu muttered as she felt his chest under her hands.

"Ew, I think Grandpa Magnus is hooking up with Mistress Neferu," Graydon whispered to the class, looking first to Tara and then to his sister.

"Duh. They're total True Loves. They have been forever," Helena told them as they all now peered out the window of the classroom door. "They just needed a little push."

"That was you?" Tara giggled. "I thought it was Agnes or Vilma who tripped Neferu."

Helena smiled and felt the surge of the Goddess flow through her. Yes, she was the balance between good and evil. Yes, she had inherited her mother's fifth element. Yes, her father would destroy any date she brought home. However, that didn't mean she didn't like to play matchmaker. There was nothing the Goddess enjoyed more than spreading love.

"Who's that?" Ellis asked.

Helena turned to see a new kid walking down the hall. His streaky blond hair was long and a little shaggy. His eyes were a piercing blue. He was tall, almost as tall as her father, and as muscled as a warrior. He had to be a year or two younger than her since she was the first born witchling in forever, but he looked at least fifty in witch years compared to her sixteen. She felt all the air leave her lungs. Oh boy. Her father was going to have a major problem with this.

Zoey pulled out the last chair at the table. Slade leaned over and took her hand in his the moment she sat down at the large table she'd placed in front of the bakery. Every morning after getting the kids to school, they all gathered together for breakfast. Slade, Zoey, Polly, Samuel, Galen, and Jane all shared this time together before Jane and Galen popped back to the stones for the rest of the day.

All around them, people and witches waved and said good morning. Zoey squeezed Slade's hand and smiled. They were so happy.

"I heard there's to be a dance tonight after the meeting.

It was all Catherine was talking about on the way to school," Polly told the group.

Jane looked down at her phone and smiled. "Tara just said Graydon asked her to it."

"About time," Slade said with a smirk. "We all know they're True Loves."

"I don't know. They're so young," Galen said a little uneasily.

"You're so lucky your daughter keeps you in the loop," Polly said. "I get some details, but not much. Mostly I get eye rolls from Catherine."

"So many eye rolls," Zoey laughed.

"Oh, and some new water witch from Sweden named Vatten Kraft asked Helena," Jane said, not looking up from her phone.

"Like hell!" Slade yelled, surprising the people walking by them on the street. "No one is taking my sweetling to a dance! Especially not some new guy. Those water power boys all think they're so smooth."

Zoey, Jane, and Polly shared a look and then burst out laughing.

"We should enter Moody Moonshine as our flavor of the year," Zoey said, still laughing. "If only we can capture the taste of moody teenagers."

"Don't think you'll be winning this year," Peach said as she and her husband stopped by the table. "The Irises are going to take you down."

Otis shook his head. "The Opossums are going to win flavor of the year."

"Are y'all talking about the Moonshine Flavor of the Year?" Maribelle asked as she and Dale joined them. "Don't even think about it. The Mountaineers are going to win this year. Hands down."

"Aren't you all getting close to aging out of the Mountaineers?" Peach asked.

"Married seventeen years," Dale said, lacing his hand through Maribelle.

"Young'uns," Otis muttered to Peach before he placed a kiss on her cheek. "Let's show these whippersnappers how to make real moonshine."

"Are you suggesting an Iris and Opossum joint flavor?" Peach asked with a gasp.

Otis and Peach scurried off with their heads together.

"I'd hate to tell them they have nothing to worry about since Moody Moonshine would taste like unwashed clothes and overused cologne," Polly said with a snort.

Zoey and the rest of the table broke out into belly laughs. This was Moonshine Hollow. A small town filled with witches and humans living together. A magical town where nothing was secret, the moonshine was strong, and the love stronger.

THE END

Forever Concealed

Forever Devoted

Forever Hunted

Forever Guarded

Forever Notorious

Forever Ventured

Forever Freed

Forever Saved

Forever Bold

Forever Thrown

Forever Lies (coming Jan/Feb 2022)

Shadows Landing Series

Saving Shadows

Sunken Shadows

Lasting Shadows

Fierce Shadows

Broken Shadows

Framed Shadows

Endless Shadows

Fading Shadows (coming April/May 2022)

Women of Power Series

Chosen for Power

Built for Power

Fashioned for Power

Destined for Power

ABOUT THE AUTHOR

Kathleen Brooks is a New York Times, Wall Street Journal, and USA Today bestselling author. Kathleen's stories are romantic suspense featuring strong female heroines, humor, and happily-ever-afters. Her Bluegrass Series and follow-up Bluegrass Brothers Series feature small town charm with quirky characters that have captured the hearts of readers around the world.

Kathleen is an animal lover who supports rescue organizations and other non-profit organizations such as Friends and Vets Helping Pets whose goals are to protect and save our four-legged family members.

Email Notice of New Releases

https://kathleen-brooks.com/new-release-notifications

Kathleen's Website
www.kathleen-brooks.com
Facebook Page
www.facebook.com/KathleenBrooksAuthor
Twitter
www.twitter.com/BluegrassBrooks
Goodreads
www.goodreads.com

Made in United States
Orlando, FL
20 February 2022